CRIME AND PUNISHMENT

CRIME AND PUNISHMENT

Fyodor Dostoyevsky

Om KIDZ
An imprint of Om Books International

First published in 2021

Om KIDZ | Om Books International

Corporate & Editorial Office
A-12, Sector 64, Noida 201 301
Uttar Pradesh, India
Phone: +91 120 477 4100
Email: editorial@ombooks.com
Website: www.ombooksinternational.com

Sales Office
107, Ansari Road, Darya Ganj,
New Delhi 110 002, India
Phone: +91 11 4000 9000
Email: sales@ombooks.com
Website: www.ombooks.com

Retold by Swayam Ganguly

ISBN: 978-93-85031-51-9

Printed in India

10 9 8 7 6 5 4 3 2 1

Contents

Chapter One

The Old Woman

On a hot evening, a young man emerged from his lodging house. He avoided meeting his landlady on the staircase. His rooms were under the roof of a high, five-storied house, resembling a cupboard more than a room. The landlady resided below, and he had to pass her kitchen each time he went out, the door of which was always open. He was scared and ashamed as he did not want to bump into his landlady, being heavily in debt to her.

The young man was not a coward, but his irritation had made him almost hypochondriac. Because of his poverty,

he had chosen to become a recluse. The young man preferred to sneak away like a cat. He did not wish to be pestered for the rent or be threatened. Neither did he want to lie or make excuses. As he slipped out, his fears were magnified. *How can I attempt a thing like THAT if I let these small things trouble me?* he thought. The heat in the Petersburg street was oppressive. The stench and the dust added to the young man's already oversensitive nerves. His refined face reflected disgust for his surroundings. He was an exceptionally handsome, tall and well-built young man with lovely dark eyes and dark brown hair, yet shabbily dressed despite his good looks.

He was also very weak as he had barely eaten for two days. "German hatter!" a drunk shouted at him from a wagon that went past. The young man clutched at his hat, a specimen of Zimmerman's, though torn and tattered with age.

Yes! he thought. *My hat is too noticeable. It's absurd and stands out. Why, it might spoil the whole plan! I should wear a cap with my rags. This hat would be remembered by most people, giving them a clue.*

His destination was a mere seven hundred and thirty steps from his lodging house. He was in feverish excitement as he approached a huge house overlooking the canal on one side and the street on the other. This house was let out in small tenements to all sorts of working people, with three to four doorkeepers. The young man sneaked inside and reached the fourth storey. He was aware that this flat had been let out to a German clerk. Now, after the exit of the German family, the fourth floor of this staircase would be uninhabited, except for the old woman residing there.

Now, that's a good thing, he thought as he rang the bell of the old woman's flat. Soon, the door was opened partially as the old woman eyed her visitor through a small crack in the door.

At first only her eyes were visible through this crack, but she became bolder seeing so many people outside, and opened the door wider for the young man to enter.

The old woman stared at the young man in silence. Her colourless hair was thickly smeared with oil. Her neck was thin and long, covered with a flannel rag and resembling a hen's leg. She wore an old fur cape despite the heat and coughed at every instant.

"Raskolnikov," the young man spoke politely. "A student. I came here a month ago."

"I remember your coming here very well, my good sir," she replied.

"I have returned with the same errand," Raskolnikov continued. The old woman asked him to enter her room, and as he did, Raskolnikov scanned the room quickly to memorise its arrangement. But there was nothing special in the room except the old furniture. Everything in the room was clean, polished and shining. There was not a spot of dust in the entire flat.

"Lizaveta's work," Raskolnikov thought. *"Such cleanliness can be found in the homes of spiteful old widows."*

He stole a quick, curious glance at the old woman's bedroom separated by another door with a curtain. These two rooms made up the entire flat.

"What do you want?" the old woman asked him severely now.

"I have something to pawn," Raskolnikov stated, withdrawing an old-fashioned silver watch from his pocket.

"But the time for your last pledge is up. The month ended the day before yesterday."

"I shall fetch you the interest for another month," Raskolnikov stated. "Wait a little."

"But my good sir, that's for me to decide if I wish to wait or sell your pledge at once."

"How much will you give me for the watch, Alyona Ivanovna?"

"You come with trifles that are worth nothing.

I gave you two roubles for your ring last time, and one could buy a new one for a rouble and a half."

"Give me four roubles! I shall redeem it as it was my father's watch. I shall be getting some money soon."

"A rouble and a half, and interest in advance, if you want."

"A rouble and a half!" Raskolnikov exclaimed.

"Please yourself," the old woman said, handing him the watch. He took it angrily and was about to leave. Then, he checked himself suddenly.

"Hand it over!" he said roughly. The old woman fumbled in her pocket for her keys and went into the other room. Raskolnikov stood there, thinking deeply. He heard her unlocking the chest of drawers. *It must be the top drawer,* he thought. *She carried the key in her right pocket. All the keys are in a single bunch on a steel ring. There's a single key that's three times as big as the others. It has deep knotches and must be the key to some other chest. Strong-boxes have such keys.*

The old woman returned. "Here, sir," she said. "Ten copecks the rouble a month. So, I take fifteen copecks from a rouble and a half as advance for the month. I have lent you two roubles before, and so you owe me twenty copecks in advance now. That makes thirty-five copecks in total. Here is a rouble and fifteen copecks for the watch!"

The young man took the money without argument.

"Alyona Ivanovna, I might be getting you something valuable in a few days. A silver cigarette box, as soon as I get it from a friend," he declared.

"We will talk about it when you get it, sir."

"Goodbye, then. Are you always home alone? Isn't your sister with you?" he enquired casually, walking into the passage.

"What business is she of yours?"

"Oh, nothing. I just asked. Good day!"

"How loathsome the thought is!" he cried, when he was out in the street. "How can I

possibly do it? It is nonsense! My heart cannot be capable of such filthy things!"

But he was agitated and repulsed beyond belief. Unknowingly, he reached a tavern, and went down the steps to enter it. He longed for cold beer because of lack of food. As he drank the first glass, his muddled thoughts became clearer.

Chapter Two

The Man in the Tavern

The tavern had few people. Raskolnikov detested crowds normally, but now he felt this strange urge to be with people. Raskolnikov spotted a man resembling a clerk staring at him, as if eager to make conversation. He was a bald man, about fifty years old, and considered the others in the room to be inferior to him. Although he was of medium height, he was stoutly built with a face puffed because of continuous drinking.

"Honoured sir, may I engage you in polite conversation?" he enquired. "My experience tells me that you are an educated man unaccustomed

to drinking. My name is Marmeladov and I am a titular counsellor. May I be bold to enquire if you have been in the service?"

"No, I am a student," a surprised Raskolnikov replied.

"Ah! that's just what I had guessed," the man said excitedly, as he picked up his jug and glass, and seated himself next to the young man. "A student or a former student! Poverty is not a vice, dear sir. But then, drunkenness is not a virtue either. But beggary is certainly a vice! You retain your nobility of soul in poverty, but never in beggary. Tell me something, have you ever spent a night on a hay barge, on the Neva?"

"No," Raskolnikov replied. "What do you mean?"

"I have done so for the fifth night," Marmeladov replied.

Raskolnikov spotted bits of hay on the man's clothes and hat. It appeared likely that he hadn't washed or changed clothes for five days as well. Marmeladov had filthy hands

with black nails. His speech excited interest among the other occupants in the room and it was apparent that he was a regular here. The boys at the counter were sniggering, and the innkeeper descended from the upper room to hear the funny fellow speak.

"When Mr. Lebeziatnikov beat my wife, did I not suffer? Young man, have you ever asked for a loan hopelessly?" Marmeladov asked.

"Yes," Raskolnikov replied. "But what do you mean by hopelessly?"

"When you know beforehand that you won't get anything," Marmeladov explained. "Just like I know that this man won't lend me money as he knows I won't pay it back. Why should he? Out of compassion? Mr. Lebeziatnikov, a man in tune with modern ideas, explained that compassion is forbidden by science, and that is the way in England now, where there is political economy. But I had no choice but to go and ask him for money. Agreed, I am a pig, but she is a lady! My spouse, Katerina Ivanovna is an

educated woman and an officer's daughter. But only if she loved me! But she is unjust, and I am a beast," he declared, as the others guffawed, and the innkeeper yawned.

"It is my fate, dear sir," Marmeladov continued unaffected. "But I have sold her stockings as well, for drink. I have sold her mohair shawl too, and she has caught cold as we live in a cold room. She caught cold this winter and has been coughing blood. We have three little children and she works from morning to night. Do you think I don't feel the pain? The more I drink, the more I feel it. Yet, that is why I drink so that I can find feeling and sympathy in drink. I drink to suffer twice as much," he said, laying his head on the table in despair. "I see that you are troubled, young man," he continued, raising his head again. "That is why I spoke to you instantly. By telling you my story, I do not wish to make myself a laughing stock before all these idle people. I am looking for someone with education and feeling to tell my story to.

My wife was an educated woman from a noble family, and that is why she could not stand Mr. Lebeziatnikov being rude to her. When he beat her, she went to bed because her self-respect was hurt more than the injury caused by the blows. When I married her, she was a widow with three small children. Her first husband beat her, and she still thinks of him fondly. When he died, all her relatives abandoned her. She was left in such poverty and suffering that I offered to marry her, being a widower with a fourteen-year-old daughter. She married me as she did not have a choice. When I could not please her for a year, I took to drink. My daughter Sonia has grown up now but had a lot of trouble with Katerina Ivanovna, who is a generous, but short-tempered lady. Sonia has had no education despite all my attempts to get her educated. Tell me, how much can a respectable, poor girl earn these days? Sonia could not earn more than fifteen farthings a day and was constantly rebuked by my wife for not earning enough. Katerina Ivanovna blamed as her little children were starving. So, Sonia went to Darya Frantsovna, an evil woman well known to the police. She had tried to get my daughter do evil things before and had failed. Sonia left at six in the evening and returned at nine to lay thirty roubles before Katerina Ivanovna in silence. Then, Sonia lay down on the bed facing the wall, her body shuddering. Katerina Ivanovna went to the bed and hugged Sonia, and they fell asleep in each other's arms. Since then, my daughter has been forced to take a yellow ticket and cannot live with us anymore, as our landlady would not permit it. The problems between Mr. Lebeziatnikov and Katerina Ivanovna were also because of Sonia. He refused to live in the same rooms with a girl like Sonia, and Katerina stood up for Sonia and got beaten up. Now, Sonia visits us mostly after dark, and gives Katerina Ivanovna all she can. Sonia lives in a room with the poor tailors Kapernaumovs, although her room is partitioned. Then I got this job, and everything changed. I was treated with more respect by my wife and family. Then, one day, I stole the key of Katerina Ivanovna's box, took whatever was there of my earnings, and left home. It's been five days now, and my employment has been terminated."

Raskolnikov agreed to accompany Marmeladov to his house upon being invited. The two men reached the house and went up to the fourth storey. Raskolnikov recognised Katerina Ivanovna instantly, who was pacing agitatedly up and down the room. She was about thirty years old and certainly seemed a strange wife for Marmeladov. The youngest child, a girl of six was asleep on the sofa. The boy, a year older had probably received a beating, and was being comforted by his nine-year-old sister. Katerina Ivanovna screamed on spotting her husband on his knees at the door. "The monster has returned? But where is the money?" She yelled and started searching his pockets. "The Lord have mercy on us! Has he drunk it all?"

Enraged, she grabbed him by the hair inside the room. Marmeladov offered no resistance, meekly crawling along. The youngest child woke up and started crying. Her elder brother screamed and ran into his elder sister's arms who was shaking like a leaf.

"They are hungry!" she pointed at the children. Then, she attacked Raskolnikov. "You've been drinking with him? Go away!"

The young man was leaving when the inner door was flung open. Curious faces peered inside; coarse faces that laughed, smoking pipes and cigarettes with heads that wore caps. Inside the room were women of questionable character, who entered this room now, led by Amalia Ivanovna, who restored order among her own kind. Then, she scared the poor woman for the hundredth time by abusing her in filthy language to vacate the premises the next day. Just before he left, Raskolnikov laid down all the coppers he had with him on the window, unnoticed.

Chapter Three

A Mother's Letter

Raskolnikov woke up late the next day but hadn't slept well. He surveyed his small, cupboard-like room with hatred. Not only were the walls peeling off, but the room was so low-ceilinged that a very tall man would bump his head against the ceiling. All the furniture that existed here were three old and rickety chairs, an old, dusty table covered with books, and an ancient sofa that served as the young man's bed. Raskolnikov wanted to be completely alone, and even the sight of the cook and servant girl, Nastasya, irritated him now. He dismissed her

after she fetched him some soup and a letter. The letter was from his mother. Raskolnikov grew weak as it had been long since he had received a letter. Besides, an unknown fear worried his heart. After Nastasya left, he opened the letter with shaking hands.

My dear Rodya, his mother wrote- *It's two months since your last letter, that distressed me, and kept me awake all night, thinking. But I know you won't blame me for this silence, as you know I love you and you are all Dounia and I have. It was such a shock to me when I heard that you have given up the university a few months ago because of lack of means to support yourself. How could I help you with my pension of a hundred and twenty roubles a year? I borrowed the fifteen roubles I sent you four months ago, on the security of my pension. I had to wait till the debt was repaid off and that has just happened, and I could not send you more money. But I will be able to send you something now and let us congratulate ourselves on our good fortune. If I had revealed to you about Dounia's sufferings earlier, I feared that you would leave everything and come to us. Dounia received a hundred roubles as advance when she took the position of governess in the Svidrigailov family, on the condition that the money be deducted from her salary every month. So, although she faced many insults, it was impossible for her to leave the job without repaying the debt. She took this job to send you the sixty roubles that you needed so desperately then. We lied to you, by saying that the money came from Dounia's savings. Everyone in the house was nice to Dounia, except Mr. Svidrigailov, who always insulted her. Later, we learnt that he had developed a passion for Dounia, that he hid by being rude to her, being ashamed of his passion. But he lost control eventually, and made indecent proposals to Dounia, asking her to move to another estate of his where he could be alone with her. But Dounia bore it all as she needed the money and wanted the family to avoid a scandal. But one day, Marfa Petrovna overheard her husband imploring to Dounia in the garden. She blamed Dounia for everything. Not only did she hit Dounia but refused to listen to her explanations. She shouted at her for an hour and ordered that she be packed off in a peasant's cart. Dounia did not allow me to write to you earlier, and the entire town gossiped about this scandal. We dared not even attend Church because of the contemptuous looks we received. Marfa Petrovna slandered Dounia throughout the town, but she bore it all like an angel. Thankfully, a repentant Mr. Svidrigailov confessed his sins to his wife, and although Marfa Petrovna was crushed, she wept and embraced Dounia. Then, she went all around town proclaiming Dounia's innocence although this disgraced her husband. Dounia was treated with great respect, and she has agreed to marry a*

suitor. Although this has been done without your consent, I hope you will not be angry with us. He is a counsellor named Pyotr Petrovitch Luzhin, and a distant relation of Marfa Petrovna, who was instrumental in bringing this match about. He is respectable and presentable, although a little conceited. But although he is forty-five, he is respectable and has made his fortune. But I thought it was rude of him to say that he had always wanted to marry a poor girl as it was better for a wife to be indebted to her husband than the other way around. But Dounia thinks it is a good match, and both of us think he could be very useful for you to advance your career. Dounia and I will leave for Petersburg as he is eager to have the ceremony done as soon as possible. I send you a mother's blessing till we meet again. Love your sister Dounia as she loves you more than herself.

Yours till death,
Pulcheria Raskolnikov

Raskolnikov's face had been wet with tears as soon as he had started reading the letter. But after he finished, his face was pale and twisted. His brain was in a turmoil, and he decided to go out for some fresh air as he was cramped in that little room. The passers-by were stunned when he spoke to himself as he walked. Most thought he was drunk!

Chapter Four

The Girl on the Street

This marriage won't take place while I am alive, Raskolnikov thought angrily. "It's a marriage that's mutually beneficial. The businessman has got the better of them. But how could Dounia, of all people, allow herself to be sold like this? Or is this her sacrifice for her mother and her brother? But what will you do to prevent it? Besides, what right do you have? What can you do to promise them a better future? All you are doing now is living off them, eating up their pension. What will happen to them after ten years? I must act now or give up life altogether!" he exclaimed

in a frenzy. He recalled the desperation of Marmeladov suddenly and could relate to it.

He looked for a seat, walking along the K____ Boulevard, and spotted one a hundred paces ahead. He saw a woman walking twenty paces ahead of him and paid her no attention initially. But there was something so strange about this woman that he was forced to concentrate totally on her. She was a young girl, walking in the heat bareheaded, without gloves or parasol, waving her arms about crazily. Her silky dress was strangely worn, not properly hooked up, and was torn open at the top of the skirt, near the waist. She walked unsteadily, stumbling and swaying from side to side.

Raskolnikov overtook the girl at the seat, but she dropped down on it, closing her eyes and leaning back on the seat in great exhaustion. To his great shock, he saw that she was fully drunk. She was fifteen or sixteen, and totally unaware that she was out on the street. The

boulevard was deserted, and Raskolnikov spotted a gentleman on the further side, staring at the girl. He had followed the girl with an intent of his own, but now found Raskolnikov in the way. He stared at Raskolnikov angrily. He was a fat, thirty-year-old fashionable gentleman.

"Svidrigailov!" Raskolnikov exclaimed. "What are you doing here?"

"What do you mean?" the astonished gentleman asked haughtily.

"Get away from here, that's what I mean!"

"You low fellow! How dare you?" the gentleman raised his cane. Raskolnikov rushed at him with his bare fists. But the two were separated by a police constable, who suddenly arrived.

"Enough, gentlemen!" he ordered. "No fighting in a public place, please!"

"Who are you and what do you want?" he demanded of Raskolnikov sternly, noticing his rags suddenly. The policeman appeared to be a kind man, and Raskolnikov drew his attention towards the girl on the seat by leading him there. Svidrigailov watched from a distance. "She has been drunk and deceived," he announced to the policeman. "This man, whom I was about to fight, was trying to take advantage of her. We must keep the girl away from the man and get her home."

The policeman understood the situation instantly and was moved when he looked at the girl closely. "Why, she is only a child," he exclaimed. "One can see that she has been deceived. Where do you live lady?" he asked her. The girl opened her tired and sleepy eyes, stared blankly at him and waved lazily. Raskolnikov discovered twenty copecks in his pocket. "Here, call a cab and drive her home," he urged the policeman, who took the money. "Where do you live?" the policeman asked the girl. "Go away! They won't leave me alone," she replied. "What a shame," the policeman said sympathetically. "It's a tough job," he said to Raskolnikov as he stared him up and down. It seemed strange to him that this man was dressed in rags and still giving him money. "Missy!" he called out to the girl again. She opened her eyes suddenly, and started walking away from them, stumbling. "The shameful wretches won't leave me alone," she said. Svidrigailov followed her, walking along another avenue, his eyes on her. The policeman followed them both, assuring Raskolnikov, "Don't worry, I'll not let him have her."

"Wait!" Raskolnikov shouted behind the policeman, who turned around. "Let them be," Raskolnikov stated. "It's none of your business. Let the man have some fun."

As the stunned policeman stared at him, Raskolnikov laughed. The policeman gave him a look of contempt, thinking him to be a madman, and followed the girl. *He's taken my twenty copecks,* an angry Raskolnikov thought. *He might just take money from the other*

fellow and let him have the girl. Why did I want to interfere? Poor girl! What if my Dounia met a fate like that? But where was I going just now? He realised that he was going to visit Razumihin, his old comrade at the university. He had few friends at the university, but had got along well with Razumihin, an intelligent, handsome, good-humoured young man whom everyone was fond of. He was also boisterous and strong. Once, he had punched a huge policeman senseless. Razumihin could drink deep like a fish but could also abstain from drinking when he wished to. He loved to play pranks and sometimes went too far with them. But the best part about Razumihin was that no failure could weigh him down; he could live anywhere and fight the extreme harshness of cold and hunger. He was a very poor man, living on some menial job or the other. One whole winter, he lived without lighting his stove, and was heard to say that this was better as one slept more

soundly in the cold. Presently, he had been forced to give up the university, and was trying hard to make money so he could study again. Raskolnikov realised suddenly that he hadn't seen Razumihin for the last four months.

Chapter Five

The Dream

Raskolnikov came across a tavern and entered it. He ate a pie and drank a glass of vodka. When he left the tavern, he felt drowsy as he had consumed vodka after a long time. He travelled homewards but fell asleep on the grass. Such was his mental condition that Raskolnikov had a terrible dream. He was back in his childhood in his hometown. He was seven years old, taking an evening walk with his father in the country. A corpse resembling a dark blur lay on the edge of the horizon on this heavy day. He saw the familiar tavern which had always

caused aversion and fear whenever he crossed it with his father. Drunken, horrible figures slouched in this tavern, and he used to cling on to his father fearfully whenever he saw them. A winding, dusty road from the tavern led to the graveyard. A stone church with a green cupola stood in the middle of this graveyard. He used to attend mass twice or thrice a year with his parents when a service was held in memory of his grandmother. She had long been dead, and he had never seen her. His little brother's grave was right next to his grandmother's grave. He had died when he was six months old.

Raskolnikov used to kiss his brother's grave whenever he visited. Now, in his dream he was walking towards the graveyard with his father. As he crossed the tavern fearfully, something arrested his attention. Festivities were in progress, with drunk men and women celebrating. A strange cart stood at the entrance of the tavern, and a small old mare was attached to it. Suddenly, many big, drunken peasants exited the tavern. "Get in!" a young thick-necked peasant exclaimed. He had a fleshy face just like a carrot. "I'll take you all!" Everyone laughed. "Take us all with a beast like that. You are crazy to put a nag like that, Mikolka."

"I'll make her gallop!" Mikolka boasted.

"Gallop? She hasn't done so for the last ten years!"

"She'll jog along. Just get a whip each."

"All right! Give it to her!"

Six men climbed onto the cart, and there was room for more. A fat, rosy-cheeked woman was hauled up. They were all laughing. The mare pulled with all her might, but could not move, forget gallop. Mikolka flew into a rage and started lashing the mare with his whip. There were mild protests from the crowd, but Mikolka insisted that the mare was his property, and rained further blows. There was laughter from the crowd when the mare started kicking weakly to counter the blows. Mikolka and his friends started beating the mare savagely, and a young Raskolnikov started crying.

"I'll teach you to kick," Mikolka exclaimed. He picked up a long, thick shaft from the bottom of the cart and hit the mare with it. Six whips descended on the mare as well, as the shaft descended four times.

"She's a tough one," someone said. Mikolka was furious that he could not kill the mare with a single blow. He picked up an iron crowbar and hit the mare twice. The mare fell in a heap on the ground. "Finish her off!" Mikolka shouted, and many drunken young men picked up poles, whips and sticks and ran to the mare. The mare finally breathed his last. "You are not a Christian," many voices in the crowd accused Mikolka.

But the poor boy was screaming, hugging and kissing the dead mare now. He suddenly

attacked Mikolka with his little fists but was pulled back by his father and carried away. "Father!" he wept. "Why did they kill the poor horse?" "They are drunk brutes," his father replied. "It's none of our business."

He was choked! He screamed, and woke up, perspiring and gasping for breath. "Thank God it was just a dream!" Raskolnikov exclaimed. "But good God! Can it really be that I shall strike her on the head with an axe, and steal her money? I know I can never bring myself to do it, so why I have I been torturing myself? Lord, show me my path!"

Raskolnikov entered the Hay Market at nine o'clock, and he saw Lizaveta Ivanovna speaking with her friends. Lizaveta was the younger sister of the old pawnbroker, Alyona Ivanovna, whom Raskolnikov had visited. She was a tall, thirty-five-year-old single woman. She was clumsy, submissive, timid, and almost idiotic; a slave to her elder sister and always in

perpetual fear of her. Alyona also beat up her younger sister. Raskolnikov overheard Lizaveta being invited by her friends the next evening at seven. When she accepted, Raskolnikov realised with a start that Alyona Ivanovna would be home alone the next evening. He rushed home like a man condemned to his death. The opportunity that had presented itself suddenly could make his plan work wonderfully.

Chapter Six

Murder He Wrote

Once, Raskolnikov had overheard a conversation about Alyona Ivanovna and her sister in a tavern after meeting the pawnbroker once. He had learnt that the old lady was filthy rich, and that Lizaveta was her half-sister, being the daughter of a different mother. Alyona treated Lizaveta like dirt and she was made to work all day and give all her earnings to her elder sister. The two men joked about killing the old woman for her money, which planted the first seeds in Raskolnikov's mind about performing this hideous crime.

Returning home, he withdrew a piece of wood from a hiding-place. A thin, smooth piece of

iron was attached to this piece of wood that resembled a cigarette case in length and width. This was put in a parcel to give to the old woman who would be distracted as she tried to open it. Then, he would strike with the axe that he would take from the kitchen and replace after the deed was done. His heart was beating like a drum as he stole the axe and concealed it under his clothes with the help of a noose. Then, he rushed to the old lady's house as it was already seven. No one answered as he rang the bell. His heart throbbed louder, and he rang the bell louder after thirty seconds. No answer! Knowing her habits well, he put his ear to the door. He heard the rustle of a skirt, and a hand on the lock. She was as close to the door inside as he was outside. She was alone and suspicious and had her ear on the door as well. Purposely, he moved away, loudly muttering something about not having the appearance of hiding. Then, he rang patiently and softly for a third time. The door was finally opened.

In his impatience, Raskolnikov made a dreadful mistake. He pulled at the door to prevent the old woman from closing it. As a result, Alyona Ivanovna was pulled outside as well. She stepped back in alarm as he advanced towards her.

"Good evening, Alyona Ivanovna," he tried speaking calmly, but his voice betrayed him and shook. "I have brought something for you," he declared. "It's best seen in the light," he added, and stormed inside the room. She ran after him, tongue unloosed. "Good lord!" she exclaimed. "What is it? Who are you?"

"It's me, Raskolnikov," he declared. "I've brought you the pledge I promised the other day."

The old woman regained her composure only when Raskolnikov threatened to go to another pawnbroker. She took the pledge and weighed it in her hands. "What is it?" she asked.

"The silver cigarette case I promised to bring you," he lied.

"But why are you so pale, and why do your hands shake?" she demanded. "Fever!" he lied again. "Your hands shake when you haven't had a thing to eat."

She turned towards the light to unwrap the parcel, and Raskolnikov withdrew the axe from beneath his coat. "Why have you tied it up like this?" she cried, and turned towards Raskolnikov, who struck her on the head with the axe with a powerful blow. She cried out faintly and fell to the floor, and he struck her again. Ensuring that she was dead, he took the keys from her pocket, and ran into her bedroom. The thought that the old woman might still be alive haunted him. He returned to confirm that she was dead! He noticed a string on her neck and pulled at it. But it would not come loose, and he cut it with the axe, smearing his hands in blood. It was a purse stuffed with money, and he pocketed it. Then, he rushed back to the bedroom, carrying the axe. In a terrible hurry, he tried opening the drawers with trembling hands. But they wouldn't open.

Then, he recalled the thought on his previous visit that the big key in the bunch was probably that of a big box, and that all the wealth was probably hidden in that box. He immediately looked under the bedstead and found a big box there. The big key fitted perfectly, and the box was unlocked. There were clothes inside, and he wiped his blood-stained hands on a red brocade immediately, thinking that it would be less noticeable there.

A gold watch suddenly slipped out from the clothes, and he discovered many articles of gold concealed between the clothes. He began cramming his trouser pockets and overcoat with the valuables, realising he did not have space to take them all. Suddenly, he heard footsteps in the room where the dead woman lay. He froze when he heard a low moan. Seizing his axe, he rushed outside. He stood face to face with Lizaveta, who began shaking like a leaf on seeing him. She was so scared that she couldn't scream. With one blow of the axe, he killed Lizaveta. Fear dominated his

senses now, and he longed to run away from the place. But he washed the axe and his hands with soap and water first. Then, he had just finished cleaning the axe with a cloth when he heard footsteps and voices on the staircase. He quickly fastened the door that he had forgotten to lock and waited. He was struck with terror when the two men, looking for the pawnbroker, pulled at the fastened door. Thankfully, it did not give way. Then, one man remained at the door while the other went to fetch the porter. After some time, the second man grew impatient of waiting and walked down the staircase. Raskolnikov chose this moment to make his escape, relieved that no one saw him leave. He replaced the axe in its original place when he returned, and sank into his sofa, millions of thoughts swarming in his brain.

Chapter Seven

The Fiancé

Raskolnikov could not sleep! He realised it was past two o'clock when he heard the drunks exiting the taverns. He jumped up as he recollected everything. He saw remnants of blood on his trousers and cleaned them. He shoved the stolen things inside a hole in the wall. Then, he destroyed all the evidence that could connect him with the crime. Then, tiredness overcame him, and he slept off on the sofa again.

Raskolnikov was woken up by Nastasya banging on the door. He opened the door to see her standing with the porter. *All is discovered!* were his first thoughts. To confirm, the porter

told him that he had been summoned to the police office and handed him a paper sealed with bottle-wax.

If they question me, I'll confess everything, Raskolnikov thought as he neared the police station. The clerk directed him to the head clerk, and Raskolnikov entered a room full of people. He was relieved that he had been summoned because he had not paid his long overdue rent, and not as a murder suspect. He was questioned and eventually released. *They suspect me!* he thought as he walked outside. *There will be a search immediately.*

His former terror had returned to dominate him again. But he discovered that no one had searched his room when he reached. But how could he have left the stolen things in that hole? He panicked and thought. *I shall fling them all into the canal!*

But this plan could not be executed as someone or the other was always around at the bank of the Ekaterinisky Canal. Finally, he buried the

loot in a hole under a huge stone, weighing sixty pounds, in a garbage area.

A relieved Raskolnikov walked for a long time endlessly and reached Razumihin's house without realising it. Razumihin was convinced that his friend had lost his sanity, and an angry Raskolnikov left his house. Back home, at night he heard sounds of the assistant superintendent of police beating up his landlady. "Why is the assistant superintendent beating up the landlady?" he asked Nastasya when she arrived with some food and urged him to eat.

"No one beat the landlady," she stated, and the way she looked at him, scared Raskolnikov.

He was in a state of fever and delirium and imagined people had come to take him away. He flew into fits of rage, terror and forgetfulness. Then, at ten in the morning, a stranger visited him with Nastasya. He was a young, bearded man, and had been sent by his company to remit thirty-five roubles to Raskolnikov on behalf of his mother. "It's good you have come to your senses," Razumihin said to Raskolnikov after the stranger left. "You haven't eaten or drunk anything for four days, and we gave you tea in spoonfuls. Zossimov examined you to declare that some nervous nonsense had gone to your head because of bad feeding."

Razumihin fed Raskolnikov with spoonfools of tea till he was strong enough to sit up on the sofa. He informed Raskolnikov that his debts had been cleared, with his own money of course. Then, Zossimov, a tall, fat man, a young medical practitioner and friend, arrived to see how Raskolnikov was doing.

"Do you know that that old pawnbroker woman was murdered?" Razumihin declared. "A house-painter called Nikolay has been accused of the murder. We're trying to save him as I'm convinced that he is innocent."

"A painter?" Raskolnikov asked.

"Lizaveta was murdered as well," Nastasya added.

"Lizaveta!" Raskolnikov whispered.

"Was there any evidence against the painter?" Zossimov asked.

"Evidence that was hardly evidence, and that is what we are trying to prove," Razumihin replied. "By the way," he addressed Raskolnikov. "The murders happened the day before you fainted at the police office when they spoke about it."

Zossimov stared curiously at Raskolnikov.

"The painter was arrested when he tried to sell some jewels which he claimed he found on the street," Razumihin continued.

Suddenly, a stranger entered and asked for Raskolnikov.

"I am Pyotr Petrovitch Luzhin," he said. Raskolnikov had no clue who the man was. But when he mentioned his mother and sister, Raskolnikov cried out, "So you are the fiancé?" Luzhin was offended, but informed Raskolnikov that his mother and sister were expected in town any moment, and he had obtained lodgings for them nearby. The conversation then shifted to the murders again, and Luzhin opined that crime

had been on the rise among the lower classes in Russia during the last five years.

"But peasants don't pawn trinkets," Razumihin opposed him. "What if the pawnbroker has been murdered by someone belonging to a higher class?"

"Economic ideas cannot lead to murder, and one can only think that...," Luzhin said, and was interrupted rudely by Raskolnikov.

"But didn't you tell your would-be wife that what pleased you most was that she was a beggar, and that it was better to raise a wife from poverty so that you had complete control over her?" he said savagely.

"You distort my words," Luzhin exclaimed. "The news that has been conveyed to you is false. Your mother has misinterpreted my speech."

"If you ever speak a word about my mother, I shall send you flying downstairs," Raskolnikov threatened. An offended Luzhin left immediately. Raskolnikov asked to be left alone, and Zossimov persuaded Razumihin to leave. "I think the idea

of his sister marrying that man has upset him," Razumihin declared.

"But the very mention of the murders seems to upset him," Zossimov stated, and Razumihin agreed. "He even fainted at the police station when it was being spoken about."

"It is very interesting," Zossimov said. "I shall go and see him again after half an hour."

Chapter Eight

Revisiting the Scene of the Crime

After his friends left, Raskolnikov dressed in the new clothes that Razumihin had brought him and took the twenty-five roubles that was left of his money. In a minute, he was on the street. It was eight o'clock, and the sun was setting. He was weak and dizzy as he headed towards Hay Market. He entered a restaurant and asked for tea and the newspapers. Scanning the newspaper, he finally found what he was looking for, and read eagerly.

Suddenly, someone joined him at his table. It was the head clerk Zametov, and he was a bit drunk. "You here?" he exclaimed in

surprise. "How strange! Razumihin told me only yesterday that you were unconscious. Are you aware that I had been to see you?"

Raskolnikov knew Zametov would come to see him. He smiled, and there was an irritable impatience in that smile.

"Your friend Razumihin is a hot head. But you seem delirious. You shouldn't have come out. What are you reading in the papers?" Zametov demanded.

"I was looking for the news of the murder of the old pawnbroker," Raskolnikov whispered, bringing his face close to Zametov, surprising him. "The same old woman whom you were speaking about in the police office when I fainted. Do you understand now?"

"What do you mean?" an alarmed Zametov asked, and Raskolnikov broke out in nervous laughter.

"You are either mad…or," Zametov began, and then stopped, as if stunned by the thought that crossed his mind.

"What?" Raskolnikov demanded. "Tell me!"

"Nothing! It's all nonsense. But what is clear is that the murderer was desperate. He risked everything but failed to rob the place."

"Why didn't you catch him then?"

"They will."

"You have a tough job on your hands. But if he has money now, he must be spending it. That must be the lead."

"They always do that," Zametov replied. "A man will commit a murder and then go drinking in a tavern. But not all are as cunning as you are. You wouldn't go to a tavern, would you?"

"This is what I would have done," Raskolnikov replied. "I would have taken the money to a deserted place and buried it under a heavy stone. I wouldn't touch the money for two to three years."

"You are a madman," Zametov whispered, turning away from Raskolnikov. "But what if I had murdered the old woman and Lizaveta?" Raskolnikov whispered.

"But is that possible?" Zametov asked weakly.

"But you did believe it, didn't you?"

"Never. I don't believe it even now."

"But you did believe it before then?"

"No!" an embarrassed Zametov said. "Have you been scaring me to come to this?"

"But that is what you spoke behind my back at the police office when I left."

Raskolnikov asked for the bill, and as he paid, displayed the notes in his hand to Zametov. "See how much money I have. Where did I get the money? How did I wear new clothes? You are aware that I didn't possess a single copeck after questioning my landlady. Goodbye!"

Raskolnikov exited the restaurant, and bumped into Razumihin outside, who was very angry because Raskolnikov had ventured outside in his present state. The two argued again. Raskolnikov left his friend to walk to X_Bridge. He felt so weak that he rested on the railing. Suddenly, he spotted a tall woman on his right

side. Without warning, she stepped over the railing, and threw herself into the canal. "A woman drowning!" people shouted, and soon the bridge was crowded. The woman was saved by a policeman who pulled her out of the water. "It's our Afrosinya," a woman cried. "She's drunk out of her senses. We cut her down the other day when she tried to hang herself. Here she is in trouble again!"

Raskolnikov's depression had ended. He decided to go to the police office and on the way, spotted the house of the old pawnbroker he had murdered. He entered the flat, surprised to find the door open. Two workmen were papering the walls with a new white paper. For some reason, Raskolnikov was annoyed. "Who are you? What do you want?" the workmen asked him when Raskolnikov started inspecting the flat. "Where is the blood?" he demanded. "There was a perfect pool here after the old woman and her sister were killed."

"But who are you?" the stunned workers

asked. "Come to the police station and I'll tell you," he replied. It was time for the workmen to leave, and Raskolnikov stepped outside with them to ask the same questions to the porter. Eventually, he was thrown out. But Raskolnikov had made up his mind. He would go to the police office and confess everything. It would all be over soon!

Chapter Nine

The Death of a Drunkard

Raskolnikov spotted an elegant carriage in the middle of the road. The coachman was outside, and a crowd had gathered, with the police at the front. Everyone was talking and shouting at the same time. Raskolnikov moved closer to see that the carriage had hit someone who was lying on the road. The injured man had to be taken to the hospital, but no one knew him.

"I know him," Raskolnikov shouted. "He's a retired government clerk named Marmeladov."

Raskolnikov's suggestion that Marmeladov should be taken home, instead of the hospital where he would die, was accepted. With

the help of a few men, he took Marmeladov home. Together, they placed him on the sofa. Katerina Ivanovna was terrified at this sight, and the children were screaming and trembling. Raskolnikov tried to calm down Katerina Ivanovna and noticed that she was not as weak as he had perceived. She put a pillow under her husband's head instantly, a thought that had crossed no one's mind. Then, she undressed him and began examining him, composing herself from screaming out.

"I've sent for a doctor," Raskolnikov kept assuring her. "I'll pay, don't worry. Get me water, and a napkin or a towel quickly now! He's just injured."

After she fetched the basin of water, almost fainting with the effort, Raskolnikov began wiping the blood off Marmeladov's face with a towel. Looking at his anxious wife, Raskolnikov realised he had made a big mistake in getting the injured man here. Even the policeman stood by nervously.

Katerina Ivanovna shouted to Polenka to run to Sonia's house and fetch her. Meanwhile, almost the entire neighbourhood had gathered outside the room, and Katerina Ivanovna shouted at them because they wouldn't let a man die in peace. As she was exchanging heated words with the landlady, she was interrupted by a cough from her husband. The dying man recovered to groan, and she ran towards him. He did not recognise Raskolnikov who was hovering over him as blood oozed out of the corners of his mouth.

"My God! His chest is crushed!" Katerina Ivanovna exclaimed, and asked him to turn a bit so his clothes could be taken off.

"A priest!" he groaned softly.

"They've gone for him," she shouted, and he was silent.

Soon, his eyes sought out little Lida, his favourite, who stared at her father in great wonder.

"Barefoot!" he exclaimed, indicating Lida's feet.

"Be silent!" his irritated wife exclaimed. "You know why she is barefooted."

The doctor arrived, and after examining the wounded man's chest, found it crushed and fractured with many ribs broken. A horse had kicked him just over the heart, leaving behind a big bruise. The policeman informed him that the man was caught in the wheel and been carried for thirty yards on the road.

"It's a miracle he has recovered consciousness," the doctor stated. "He will die soon, within the next five or ten minutes."

The priest arrived, and the doctor exchanged places with him. The confession was soon over, and everyone prayed. Polenka came rushing in, and was followed by a young girl. Sonia was a frail, yet pretty eighteen-year-old girl. She had lovely blue eyes.

The priest tried consoling Katerina Ivanovna, but she had only bitter words for her husband, whom she accused of spoiling their lives for drink. Then, she emitted a hollow cough, holding her mouth with a handkerchief with one hand and her aching chest in the other. She displayed the handkerchief to the priest. It was covered with blood! The priest bowed his head silently.

Marmeladov was in his last stage and had his eyes on his wife all the time, trying in vain to say something to her. Then, his eyes fell on Sonia. "Who's that?" he exclaimed, and with supernatural strength propped himself up on his elbow, despite his wife's warnings. Suddenly, he recognised his daughter, ashamed in her humiliation and gaudy finery.

"Forgive me, Sonia! Forgive me, my daughter," he cried, holding his hand out towards her. He lost his balance, and fell off the sofa, face down. They rushed to put him back, but he was dying. Sonia rushed forward to embrace him, and he died in her arms.

Raskolnikov requested Katerina Ivanovna to repay his debt to his friend by giving him a decent burial. He offered her twenty roubles

and left. He was just descending the last steps of the staircase when Polenka caught up with him.

"What is your name and address?" she asked. "Who sent you?"

"Sister Sonia. After she sent me, mamma asked me to run fast."

Polenka hugged Raskolnikov warmly, and he gave her his name and address, promising to come the next day.

Raskolnikov headed straight to Razumihin's house who offered to drop him home. Razumihin complimented him on frightening Zametov. Raskolnikov saw a light in his room and was greatly surprised. He requested Razumihin to accompany him. Entering, he got the greatest surprise. His mother and sister were waiting for him for an hour and a half. But why had they arrived unannounced? He was still dumbstruck when they rushed to embrace him and did not lift his arms to hug them back. He just couldn't. He fainted!

Razumihin had him on the sofa in an instant, assuring his mother and sister that it was nothing. Raskolnikov's mother and sister looked at him in gratitude as they had heard from Nastasya how much he had done for Raskolnikov when he was unwell.

Chapter Ten

Brother and Sister

Raskolnikov asked his mother and sister to leave him alone, and they were alarmed. "Don't bother me," he said irritably. Razumihin offered to stay with Raskolnikov and was thanked by his mother profusely.

"Dounia," Raskolnikov addressed his sister. "I don't want you to marry that man Luzhin."

"What are you saying?" she began and checked herself immediately. "We will talk about this when you are fit to do so."

"You think I'm delirious? You are marrying him for my sake, and I won't allow that. Refuse him!"

"No! What right do you have?" an offended Dounia exclaimed.

"It's either Luzhin or me," Raskolnikov stated. "You must choose, Dounia."

"You are off your mind," Razumihin shouted angrily. He forbade Raskolnikov's mother when she wanted to ask the landlady to find lodgings near Raskolnikov. They agreed to be dropped off to their rooms, and Razumihin promised to return later with news of Raskolnikov. He was back in twenty minutes to report that Raskolnikov was sleeping soundly now. "I shall fetch Zossimov now. Then you can sleep," he declared, and ran off. The two women were suitably impressed at this display of devotion and friendship. Zossimov reassured the two ladies and was dazzled at the beauty of Raskolnikov's sister.

"That's a fetching girl," Zossimov stated lecherously to Razumihin as soon as they were outside. Razumihin grabbed him by the throat and pinned him against the wall. He warned him never to say such a thing again.

The next day, Razumihin woke up in a troubled mood. He recalled his behaviour the night before and was ashamed. By what right did he abuse the girl's fiancé if he was jealous? Being drunk was no justification! Zossimov arrived and was informed that Raskolnikov was still sleeping. The young doctor left with orders that Raskolnikov wasn't to be disturbed.

Razumihin paid a visit to the ladies who were waiting for him eagerly. They invited him to have breakfast with them. Avdotya Romanovna had a look of gratitude and friendship for him, confusing Razumihin completely, as he had expected to be greeted with scorn. He patiently answered all the questions about Raskolnikov that were posed by his mother.

"I think that you are right that my brother needs a woman's care," Dounia stated.

"But he loves no one and probably never will," Razumihin replied.

"Are you saying he's incapable of love?"

"Do you know that you are just like your brother,

in all aspects?" he blurted out, and turned red. But he was relieved when she laughed.

Razumihin apologised for having spoken rudely about Dounia's would-be husband in his drunken state. Pulcheria Alexandrovna then took Razumihin into confidence, saying that Luzhin had ordered them not to receive her son because of his mental state.

"Do what Dounia says," he advised.

"She says they must meet."

"Let us check if Raskolnikov has woken up," Razumihin suggested, and the two ladies followed him.

"He is well, quite well!" Zossimov, who had arrived ten minutes before them, announced. Raskolnikov, who was sitting on the sofa, fully dressed and cleaned, displayed no joy on seeing his mother and sister. But Raskolnikov apologised to his mother for distressing her, and then held his sister's hand quietly. Dounia reciprocated by holding his hand warmly, and in that single act, brother and sister's love was rekindled.

"I wanted to come and see you today before you came to see me," Raskolnikov informed his mother and sister. "But I was delayed because I had to wash out the blood from my clothes. I forgot to ask Nastasya to do that yesterday."

"What blood?" his mother exclaimed in alarm.

"Nothing! I met a clerk I knew who had been run over yesterday and carried him home. His blood was on my clothes," Raskolnikov explained, also stating that he was broke because he had given away all his savings to the dead man's widow. "I beg your forgiveness for it, mother," he added, seeing that Dounia didn't approve of that act.

"Roudya, anything you do must be good," his mother declared lovingly.

"Don't be too sure of that," he sneered. There was a deadly silence, and it appeared to Raskolnikov that they were all scared of him.

Yet, in their absence I appeared to love them so much, he thought.

Zossimov excused himself and left. Razumihin wanted to leave as well but was restrained by

Raskolnikov. "Listen, Dounia," Raskolnikov addressed his sister, "I must ask for your pardon for my behaviour yesterday. But I do not approve of your marriage with Luzhin. I shall not consider you my sister if you marry him."

"Brother, you suffer from a grave mistake," Dounia replied. "You seem to think that I'm sacrificing myself for the family, which is not true. I am marrying for my own sake as things are difficult for me."

She is a liar! Raskolnikov thought. *The vain creature makes us want to think that she is not marrying because of charity. Oh, they even love as if they hate! How I hate them all!*

"You lie through sheer feminine obstinacy, so that you may win against my argument," he replied. "The truth is you cannot respect a man like Luzhin and are just marrying him for his money."

Dounia lost her composure and reiterated her point strongly. "I would not marry him if I was not convinced that he would respect me,"

she declared. "It is not as if I am committing a murder, Rodya. Why do you look at me like that, Rodya? Why are you so pale?"

It looked like Raskolnikov was about to faint, but he recovered just in time, explaining that it was a bout of giddiness that had affected him suddenly.

"Well, why am I making such a fuss?" he stated. "Marry whom you like!

Raskolnikov also agreed to be present for the interview with Luzhin, only because his mother and sister insisted upon it.

Chapter Eleven

Sonia

A young girl walked into the room suddenly. It was Sonia, and initially Raskolnikov did not recognise her. In the room full of people, he sensed Sonia's humiliation because of her so called 'notorious background', as explained by Luzhin. He felt sorry for her and felt a pang in his heart as she almost retreated from the room in embarrassment.

Sonia sat down upon his request, quivering in terror as she found it unthinkable that she could sit beside the two ladies. Raskolnikov introduced Sonia to his mother and sister who gazed at Sonia in disgust and amazement.

She could not meet their eyes. She informed Raskolnikov that her mother wanted him to be present at Marmeladov's funeral service followed by lunch.

"She wants to thank you for helping us. Without your help, we wouldn't have a funeral at all."

Raskolnikov could not help being attracted to her clear blue eyes and the kindness and simplicity on her face. Sonia was eighteen but looked like a child.

"You gave us all you had yesterday," Sonia said in a loud quick whisper, as Raskolnikov being poor himself and living in poor surroundings suddenly struck her. In the silence that followed, Dounia's eyes lit up and her mother looked kindly at Sonia. Then, Pulcheria Alexandrovna excused herself, after stating that they should all have dinner together later. Razumihin was radiant as he was invited as well.

Pulcheria Alexandrovna had wanted to greet Sonia as well, but somehow couldn't manage to do it. Dounia followed her mother out shortly, but not before giving Sonia an attentive, courteous bow. A totally confused and frightened Sonia curtsied hurriedly. Her face reflected pathos and discomfort, as if Dounia's attention and courtesy were painful to her.

"Goodbye, Dounia," Raskolnikov called, following her out in the passage. "Give me your hand."

"I did give it to you, remember?" Dounia replied.

"Yes, but give it to me again," Raskolnikov stated, squeezing her fingers warmly. Dounia left happily. On the street, Pulcheria Alexandrovna voiced her concerns to Dounia about Luzhin breaking off the engagement and Sonia being the main reason for all the troubles of her son. Hadn't Luzhin warned them about her?

"That's nonsense," Dounia declared. "Luzhin is a complete slanderer!"

As Sonia said goodbye to Raskolnikov and Razumihin and left, a stranger followed her.

He was a fashionable gentleman, well-built and carrying an expensive cane. He entered the house where Sonia lodged, and greeted her. He said that they were neighbours.

"I have arrived in town only day before yesterday. Goodbye for now," he said. Sonia was silent and entered her room. She felt uneasy and ashamed.

Raskolnikov was teasing Razumihin for having a thing for Dounia as they left for Porfiry Petrovitch's house for the appointment with him, regarding Raskolnikov's claims for the items he had pawned with the murdered pawnbroker.

"You are blushing like a schoolboy!" he guffawed.

"What a pig you are!" Razumihin threatened furiously. "Not a word inside, or I'll hit you."

Porfiry Petrovitch was surprised to see Raskolnikov laughing loudly and Razumihin looking totally ridiculous. Raskolnikov subdued himself as he saw Zametov seated in a corner. Razumihin sulked by the window.

"I just called him a little Romeo, and proved it," Raskolnikov explained.

"Pig!" Razumihin muttered.

"There must be grave grounds for the accusation, as he is absolutely furious," Petrovitch laughed.

"You sharp lawyer!" Razumihin exclaimed. "Damn you all," he declared, and laughed loudly himself. Then, he introduced Raskolnikov to the lawyer, "To business then! This is my friend Rodion Romanovitch Raskolnikov, who has heard of you and wanted to make your acquaintance. He also has a matter of business with you. Zametov? What brings you here? Do you know each other?"

"What does this mean?" an uneasy Raskolnikov thought.

"Well, we met yesterday at your rooms," Zametov explained. Porfiry Petrovitch asked his visitor to be seated and explain his business. Briefly, Raskolnikov explained that he wanted to redeem the things he had pawned with the now dead pawnbroker.

"You'll have to inform the police that you have learnt of the murder, and that you wish to inform the lawyer in charge of the case that you desire to redeem your goods," Porfiry Petrovitch advised, adding, "I have been expecting you for some time."

He knows! Raskolnikov thought in panic.

"Expecting him?" Razumihin cried. "How did you know he had pledges there?"

"The ring and the watch you had pledged were wrapped up together, with your name written on top of it," Petrovitch declared to Raskolnikov. "We know everyone who had pledges there, and you were the only one who didn't show up. All the others did."

"I have been unwell," Raskolnikov explained.

"Yes, I heard that something distressed you greatly. You still look pale."

"I am not pale at all," Raskolnikov protested angrily. "I am quite well."

"When you entered that house and went up the stairs, it was past seven wasn't it?" Porfiry Petrovitch enquired.

"Yes," Raskolnikov replied, realising immediately that he should not have said so.

"Did you see a workman or two in a flat that stood open on the second storey? They were painters!"

"No, I didn't see them," Raskolnikov replied, conscious that this was a trap, and that he should not fall into it.

"What are you asking?" Razumihin shouted. "The painters were at work there on the day of the murder, and he was there three days earlier."

"Oh, I have muddled it," Porfiry Petrovitch exclaimed, slapping himself on the forehead. "I thought he would be able to tell us something."

"Well, you should be more careful," Razumihin retorted, as Raskolnikov heaved a sigh of relief.

After they left the lawyer's place, Raskolnikov walked home after parting with Razumihin to see the porter in conversation with a short man.

"Here he is himself!" the porter pointed him out.

The stranger stared at Raskolnikov attentively and walked away briskly. Raskolnikov learnt from the porter that the stranger was making inquiries about him and rushed after him. He caught up with the man, and they walked side by side for a minute without speaking a word.

"You were inquiring me of the porter?" Raskolnikov asked quietly.

The man was silent and didn't even look at Raskolnikov, who repeated his words. But this time his voice broke. The stranger raised his eyes that had a dreary, sinister look.

"Murderer!" he exclaimed.

A stunned Raskolnikov walked in silence with the stranger for a hundred paces, even though he felt a cold shiver and his legs shake. "Who is a murderer?" he whispered.

"You! You are a murderer!" the man stated emphatically, looking into Raskolnikov's eyes with a smile of triumphant hatred. Then, he turned and left as a shocked Raskolnikov stared at him. The man turned when he was fifty paces and smiled at Raskolnikov in the same manner. Raskolnikov struggled into his home and pretended to be asleep when Razumihin entered. Nastasya urged Razumihin to let Raskolnikov sleep, and they left. Raskolnikov was absorbed in deep thought as to who the stranger on the street was.

Am I going mad? he thought as he laughed like a maniac. *I can never forgive that old woman!*

Raskolnikov lost consciousness, and later, had no idea how he was out in the streets. It was late evening now, and people were returning home from work. Suddenly, he spotted a man beckoning to him from the other side of the street. The man walked away as soon as Raskolnikov approached him. Raskolnikov recognised the man and was frightened. It was the very stranger who had called him a murderer!

The man entered the gateway of a large house, turned and beckoned to Raskolnikov again, who followed the man inside to climb

up the staircase. As the moon shone through the panes with a dark and mysterious light, Raskolnikov recognised the house! But how come he hadn't recognised it earlier? Reaching the second floor he saw the flat where the painters had been at work. He reached the third storey and wondered if he should go on. Then, he saw the flat wide open, hesitated momentarily, and entered. He saw the old woman sitting on the chair in the corner and withdrew the axe to strike her a blow on the head. But strangely, she did not stir. It was as if she was wooden! Then, she laughed noiselessly at him, shaking with mirth! He tried to run away, but the passage was full of people who stared at him silently. He tried to scream, and then woke up!

The dream appeared to continue though, as his door was flung open and a stranger stared at him intently. Raskolnikov closed his eyes! The stranger sat down on the sofa and waited patiently. Ten minutes passed in

complete silence. Only a fly buzzed against the window-pane! Finally, it was unbearable for Raskolnikov!

"Tell me what you want!" he demanded, getting up suddenly.

"I knew you were only pretending to sleep," the stranger laughed. "Allow me to introduce myself. Arkady Ivanovitch Svidrigailov!"

Chapter Twelve

Ghosts and Men

Raskolnikov was surprised at this unexpected visit from the man he hated but had never seen before.

"I have come to meet you for two reasons," Svidrigailov stated. "I wanted to know you better as I've heard good things about you. Secondly, I come for the welfare of your sister. She is prejudiced against me right now but with your help, she will see reason."

"You think wrongly," Raskolnikov interrupted him.

"You think I persecuted a defenceless girl in my own house," Svidrigailov said. "But has it occurred to you that I'm human enough to fall in love? Tell me, am I a monster or a victim? If I wished to elope with your sister to America or Switzerland, it's clear that I had no ill intentions. I just wanted us to be happy together."

"That's not the point," Raskolnikov declared. "The point is irrespective of whether you are right or wrong, we hate you! We don't want anything to do with you. Get out!"

Svidrigailov laughed nervously. "I see there's no getting around you," he said. "If not for the incident in the garden with Marfa Petrovna, I believe everything would have turned out well."

"They say you have got rid of Marfa Petrovna!"

"I daresay my own conscience is quite at rest there. The medical diagnosis of death was apoplexy because of a bath immediately after a heavy dinner and a bottle of wine."

"I wonder why you trouble yourself about it."

"Think! I hit her with a switch just twice, and there were no marks as well. Marfa Petrovna and I rarely fought and lived happily together. I only used the whip twice in all our seven years, which is unlikely for a monster. Eight years ago, I belonged to a set of men from the best of Russian society," Svidrigailov began his story, "We were men of breeding; poets, painters and men of property. I deteriorated after I arrived in the country and ended up in prison for debt. Then, Marfa Petrovna arrived, and bought me for thirty thousand silver pieces although I owed seventy. She took me to the country with her, and we married even though she was five years older than me. I couldn't leave the country for seven years as she held a document over me, the I.O.U. for thirty thousand roubles that held me captive."

"But if it wasn't for that, would you have escaped from her?"

"I don't think I wanted to go anywhere else," Svidrigailov confessed. "Neither did I want to go abroad with her, as I found it sickening. Almost a year ago, Marfa Petrovna returned the document

to me along with a considerable amount of money, saying how much she trusted me."

"It seems you are missing her."

"Maybe I am. By the way, do you believe in ghosts?" Svidrigailov enquired.

"Do you see ghosts?"

"Marfa Petrovna is pleased to visit me," Svidrigailov declared, smiling strangely.

"What do you mean?"

"She has come thrice; once on the day of the funeral, just three hours after being buried. The second time was day before yesterday, at dawn when I was travelling here. The third time was at my lodgings here just two hours ago. She speaks to me for a minute and then leaves."

"What does she speak to you about?"

Svidrigailov told Raskolnikov how Marfa Petrovna reminded him to wind the dining-room clock on her first visit as a ghost. "I've wound that clock every week for seven years, and when I forgot she would always remind me," he said. "The second day she

arrived at the station holding a pack of cards when I was leaving to come here. She was great hand at telling fortunes and asked me if I wanted my fortune for the journey told. I ran away in fright! Today, when she arrived I told her that I wanted to get married again as I didn't want her to irritate me with such trifles. She retorted saying that I wasn't setting a good example wanting to get married as soon as my wife was dead. She said she was sure that I wouldn't make a good choice of a wife, and both of us would be unhappy and that I would be a laughing-stock. Then, she left!"

"Maybe you are lying!"

"I rarely lie!" Svidrigailov replied thoughtfully.

"Have you seen ghosts before?"

"Yes, but only once. Six years ago, I had a servant called Filika. Just after his burial, I called out for him forgetfully. He entered and went to fetch my pipe. I thought he was doing it out of revenge as we had quarrelled violently just before his death. I angrily

ordered him to get out and he left, never to return again."

"You should see a doctor," Raskolnikov offered.

"I know I'm unwell, without your telling me that," Svidrigailov replied. "But I'm five times stronger than you are. You don't believe that ghosts exist?"

"No!" Raskolnikov cried out angrily.

"I think ghosts only appear before the sick," Svidrigailov stated. "But just because they can't appear before the healthy, doesn't mean that they don't exist! When a man is ill, the normal earthly organism of the world is broken, and the man encounters the other world, as in he begins to believe in the existence of the other world. This makes it easier for ghosts to establish contact. As soon as the man dies, he steps right into the other world. If you believe in a future life, you should believe this too."

"I don't believe in a future life," an irritated Raskolnikov insisted. "Please tell me why you have visited me as I have to leave."

"Yes, I have come here because your sister is to be married to Luzhin, Pyotr Petrovitch," Svidrigailov said. "However, he is no match for Avdotya Romanovna, who I believe is sacrificing herself for the welfare of her family. From whatever I had heard of you, I had gathered that you would be happy that this alliance was broken off. I am convinced now that I have met you personally."

"Your assumption is naïve, almost impudent," Raskolnikov stated.

"If you think I am furthering my own interests, you are mistaken," Svidrigailov replied. "I am just concerned about the welfare of your sister. I wish to gift her ten thousand roubles for the unpleasantness that I caused her."

"How dare you!" Raskolnikov exclaimed angrily.

"Your anger is justified," Svidrigailov said. "But this money is not a compensation for the hurt caused to your sister but out of a genuine desire of doing something to help her. I offered her much more just five weeks ago, but she chose to marry Luzhin instead, and that too for money only. Don't be angry! Think over it!"

Svidrigailov requested Raskolnikov to arrange an audience with his sister. If he didn't do so, Svidrigailov would be forced to try and meet Dounia himself.

"I'll see. Don't be too hopeful about it though," Raskolnikov replied.

"Before I leave, I would like to tell you that Marfa Petrovna left three thousand roubles in her will for your sister," Svidrigailov declared. "Avdotya Romanovna shall receive the money in two to three weeks."

As Svidrigailov left, he passed Razumihin in the doorway.

"Who was that?" Razumihin asked Raskolnikov as soon as the two rushed to reach Luzhin. Raskolnikov told him everything, adding that Dounia must be guarded from Svidrigailov. They arrived to see Luzhin waiting for them, and the three entered to meet Raskolnikov's mother and sister. There was silence after some small talk, as Luzhin did not like Razumihin's presence.

"Marfa Petrovna is dead, have you heard?" Dounia declared.

"Yes, I have heard," Luzhin replied. "I have also received information that Svidrigailov set off for Petersburg hastily just after her funeral."

"What? Here?" Dounia exclaimed and looked at her mother in alarm.

"Yes, and obviously with some plan as his haste explains," Luzhin replied.

"Good heavens!" Pulcheria Alexandrovna exclaimed. "Won't he let Dounia live in peace even here?"

"Unless you wish to meet him, I don't believe you have any cause for concern," Luzhin stated. "I am on my guard myself and trying to discover where he is residing."

"What a fright you have given me," Pulcheria Alexandrovna exclaimed. "I am sure he is responsible for Marfa Petrovna's death."

"Marfa Petrovna was unfortunate enough to fall in love with him and repay his debts eight years ago," Luzhin informed. "But for that, a criminal like him would have been sentenced to Siberia. Now, he might fall back on his old homicidal ways!"

"Good heavens!" Pulcheria Alexandrovna exclaimed.

"Do you have good evidence of this?" Dounia enquired.

"I'm only repeating what Marfa Petrovna told me in the strictest confidence," Luzhin replied. "A mysterious foreigner woman named Resslich lends small sums of money at interest, and I believe Svidrigailov has an association with this woman for a long time. Resslich had a niece, a deaf and dumb fifteen-year-old girl. Resslich hated her and beat her mercilessly. One day, the girl was discovered hanging in the garret. Investigations hinted at suicide, but later information was received that the child had been outraged by Svidrigailov. Then, you

must have heard about the servant Philip, who died because of ill-treatment."

"I heard Philp hanged himself," Dounia replied.

"Yes, but what provoked him to suicide was the cruelty of Svidrigailov," Luzhin insisted.

"Well, all I heard was that Philip was a weird man, as the servants used to say," Dounia replied.

"He was a domestic philosopher and was mocked by Svidrigailov more than hit by him."

"Avdotya Romanovna, I see you are defending Svidrigailov suddenly," Luzhin observed, smiling mysteriously. "I only wish to advise you and your mother. I think the man will end up in debtor's prison again. I am sure Marfa Petrovna has left him a pittance, well knowing the monster he was. He will resort to his old ways again."

"I beg you not to speak about Mr. Svidrigailov," Dounia insisted. "It makes me miserable."

"He has just been to meet me," Raskolnikov broke his silence.

Everyone in the room exclaimed, and Raskolnikov told everyone how Svidrigailov was keen on meeting Dounia, and how Marfa Petrovna had left Dounia three thousand roubles in her will.

"What does he want to speak to Dounia about?" Pulcheria Alexandrovna asked Raskolnikov.

"I'll tell you later," he replied. Luzhin was insulted Raskolnikov did not want to speak about the matter in his presence and wanted to leave now. Dounia told him to reconcile the differences he had with her brother. "I must choose between either one of you otherwise," she said. "That is something I do not wish to do."

Luzhin became more agitated when he heard this. "Love for your husband should outweigh that for your brother," he stated arrogantly. "Your son insulted me yesterday," he said to Pulcheria Alexandrovna. "He misrepresented the facts in a private conversation I had with you. He accused me of marrying a poor girl as it was more profitable in terms of moral character.

Kindly tell me what you repeated in your letter from my words to your son."

"I don't remember," Pulcheria Alexandrovna fumbled. "I repeated them as I understood them. Maybe he exaggerated."

"How could he without your instigation?" Luzhin demanded.

"If we had taken your words in a bad sense, me and Dounia wouldn't have been here," Pulcheria Alexandrovna said with dignity. "You keep blaming my son, but you have written false things about him as well."

"I don't think I have written anything false," Luzhin protested.

"You wrote that I gave money to the daughter of a man who was killed, whereas I gave it to the widow," Raskolnikov stated. "You did this to create a void between me and my family, and you included coarse descriptions about a girl's conduct. You don't even know this girl, and this is mean slander."

"Point out even one false thing in my letter.

Prove to me that you didn't throw away your money, and that the people in that family are not worthless, however unfortunate they may be," Luzhin said in his defence.

"You are not even worth the little finger of that girl whom you throw stones at," Raskolnikov replied.

"Would you let such a girl associate with your mother and sister?" Luzhin demanded.

"Yes. I made her sit down today with them!"

"Rodya!" Pulcheria Alexandrovna exclaimed as Dounia blushed.

"The question is at an end once for all," Luzhin smiled with haughty sarcasm. "I shall leave now, with the request that I be spared such meetings."

"You seem to think that we are here to do your bidding," Pulcheria Alexandrovna exclaimed. "You should display more kindness towards us as we have left everything to come to you."

"It must be Marfa Petrovna's legacy that makes you talk in this new tone," Luzhin said sarcastically.

"It appears that it's true that you were hoping that we were helpless forever," Dounia remarked irritably.

"I might also mention the secret proposal of Svidrigailov to your brother which has an agreeable interest for you," Luzhin replied.

"Good lord!" Pulcheria Alexandrovna cried.

"Aren't you ashamed now?" Raskolnikov asked Dounia.

"I am. Go away, Pyotr Petrovitch," she said angrily.

Luzhin had not anticipated such a turn of events, being totally confident about himself and his power over his helpless victims.

"Advotya Romanovna, if I leave now, after being dismissed thus, I shall never return," he warned.

"I don't want an insolent man like you to return," Dounia replied.

"You know that I can protest about this!"

"What gives you the right to speak to her like that?" Pulcheria Alexandrovna intervened. "What rights have you to protest? How can I give my Dounia to a man like you? Leave us now!"

"Your mother appears to forget that I accepted you despite your reputation in town. I see now that I have been foolish to disregard public opinion about you."

"You are a mean and spiteful man!" Dounia cried, and Raskolnikov stopped Razumihin from bashing up Luzhin.

"Leave the room now," Raskolnikov stepped up to Luzhin and looked him in the eye. "Not a word more, or..."

Luzhin stared at Raskolnikov angrily for a few seconds and left. No man had such hatred in his heart for another man as he had for Raskolnikov. Meanwhile, Raskolnikov informed his mother and sister that it was best that he should part with them for a while, as he was ill and not at peace. Despite their protests, he left. Razumihin soothed them saying Rodya needed rest to recover from his illness and promised to watch over him. From that day onwards, he assumed the role of the son and the brother.

Chapter Thirteen

Confession of a Murderer?

Raskolnikov went straight to Sonia's house on the canal bank. "I've come to you for the last time," Raskolnikov said sadly, although this was the first time he had come to see her. "Katerina Ivanovna is in consumption, and she will soon die because of it! What will happen to the children after that?"

"I don't know," Sonia exclaimed in despair.

"Polenka will meet the same fate, no doubt!"

"No!" she sobbed. "God will not allow something so terrible. God will protect her!"

"Maybe there is no God at all," Raskolnikov laughed, pacing up and down the room as

Sonia sobbed uncontrollably.

"What are you doing to me?"

"What does your God do for you?"

"He does everything."

She's a religious maniac, he thought.

He took out the New Testament in the Russian translation from the chest of drawers.

"How did you get this?" he asked.

"Lizaveta brought it for me," she replied.

Lizaveta! that's strange, he thought.

"I came to tell you something," Raskolnikov declared. "I have abandoned my family today. I have only you now. Let us go away together as we are both accursed."

"Go where?" a horrified Sonia asked.

"How do I know? All I know is that it is the same road. You don't understand? Perhaps you'll understand later. If I don't come tomorrow, you'll remember these words. In the future someday, you will realise what they mean. If I come tomorrow, I shall tell you who killed Lizaveta. Goodbye!"

As he left, Sonia was stunned. But at the same time, it never entered her head that he could have killed Lizaveta. All that crossed her mind was that Raskolnikov was terribly unhappy having abandoned his mother and sister. Sonia spent the entire night in a feverish and delirious state. On the other side of the door, which divided Sonia's room from Madame Resslich's flat, there was an empty room that was advertised to let. Svidrigailov had been standing at the door of this room, eavesdropping on the conversation between Raskolnikov and Sonia. He greatly enjoyed what he had overheard.

The next morning, Raskolnikov arrived at the department of the investigation of criminal causes for his appointment with Porfiry Petrovitch. "If two clever men who do not know each other meet for the first time, just like the two of us, it takes them half an hour to begin a meaningful conversation. Now, you are reading for the law, aren't you?" Petrovitch stated.

"Yes," Raskolnikov replied.

"Let me tell you something about our business," Petrovitch declared. "If I let a criminal be, but let him know that I know all about his crime, his constant terror will allow him to confess his crime himself. As I'm watching him constantly, he cannot even escape abroad. It's just like a butterfly flying around a candle! The criminal will worry himself to death or he will fly into my mouth, and I shall swallow him. That will be amusing, no?" Petrovitch laughed. Raskolnikov decided that silence was a better option than speech presently.

"You look pale," Petrovitch stated to Raskolnikov in genuine concern. "Shall I open the window?"

"Do not torture me like this," Raskolnikov burst out. "If you have any evidence that I am the murderer, arrest me!"

"You are ill," Petrovitch exclaimed, fetching some water. "Here, drink this! Your illness shall return like this, dear fellow! Now, I know everything! I know how you asked the

workmen and the porter about the blood in the room. We've had a similar case before, where a hallucinating man confessed to a murder he didn't actually commit. But tell me, were you delirious when you did all this?"

"No!" Raskolnikov replied. "I was perfectly in my senses."

"Now tell me this, would a criminal actually insist on being in his senses while committing a murder?"

An irritated Raskolnikov was about to leave when the door suddenly opened. Petrovitch was told that a prisoner named Nikolai wanted to declare something. Nikolai entered and confessed that he was the murderer of Alyona Ivanovna and her sister Lizaveta.

"It is not your own tale that you are telling," Petrovitch stated, and ordered Raskolnikov to leave. "I have some questions to ask you later," he said. "So, we'll meet again, won't we?"

Raskolnikov left, totally stunned at Nikolai's strange confession.

Chapter Fourteen

A Conspiracy

Luzhin had shared the details of the ugly incident with Dounia and her mother with his co-lodger, Andrey Semyonovitch Lebeziatnikov, an action he regretted later. Luzhin hated Lebeziatnikov from the very first day he had started sharing his rooms with him, a hatred that the latter shared. In a way, Luzhin was also afraid of this young clerk. He was one of the lodgers whom Amelia Ivanovna respected the most as he was not troublesome and always paid the rent on time. Both the lodgers had been invited for the funeral feast of the deceased Marmeladov. Luzhin had learned that Raskolnikov was also among the invitees.

"I do not intend to go," Lebeziatnikov stated when Luzhin brought up the subject.

"Yes, not after the thrashing you gave her a month ago!"

"That's slander and nonsense," Lebeziatnikov protested. "She attacked me with her nails and I was merely defending myself. If women are equal to men in all respects, then there should be equality in this too. But it's true that fighting is unacceptable in the future society. I am not attending the festivities because of my principles. I would have attended if a priest would have been present."

"Is it true what they say about that dead man's daughter? Do you know that delicate looking thing?" Luzhin probed.

"Yes. She is not concerned normal in our present society. But she will be in the future society where everything will be normal, voluntary and not forced. I think Sofya Semyonovna's action is a violent protest against the organisation of society, and I respect her deeply because of it."

"But I was informed that you evicted her from these lodgings!"

Lebeziatnikov was furious. "Another slander!" he cried. "That was Katerina Ivanovna's doing. Also, I had no relations with Sofya Semyonovna. I was merely developing her. She has a beautiful character!"

"Are you trying to take advantage of her fine character? He-he! Have you proved to her that modesty is nonsense?"

"How crude you are!" Lebeziatnikov remarked. "You are also foolish to misinterpret the term 'development'. Here we are striving for the freedom of women and you have just one idea in your head. Chastity and feminine modesty are useless in themselves being mere prejudices. It is up to the girl to tell me if she desires me, and if she did so, I would consider myself lucky."

"Have you ever considered giving her a present?"

"As I've said, you don't understand at all! It is another thing that she is in such a position. You simply despise her, refusing to take a humane view of her suffering. You have no idea what a character Sofya is. I am sorry she has stopped borrowing books from me as she has given up reading now. True, she cannot break free from certain foolish ideas and prejudices, but at least she comprehends that it is an insult for a woman if a man kisses her hand as the gesture is a sign of inequality."

Luzhin asked Lebeziatnikov to introduce him to Sonia as he wished to speak to her about something. A surprised Lebeziatnikov went and fetched Sonia. "Has Raskolnikov come? Is he in there?" he whispered to Lebeziatnikov.

"Yes, he is."

"I would request you not to leave the room and leave me alone with this young woman," Luzhin requested. "God knows what Raskolnikov might say about it."

Lebeziatnikov moved towards the window of the room politely.

"Sofya Semyonovna," Luzhin began. "Firstly, my excuses to your respected mother as I won't be

able to attend the dinner. Katerina Ivanovna held the place of a mother in your life too, didn't she?"

"Yes," Sonia replied.

"I had the impression that she is ill. I would be glad to be of service to her, and..."

"Allow me to interrupt you," Sonia said, rising to her feet. "Did you mention to her yesterday about the possibility of a pension for her? She told me."

"No, that's absurd," Luzhin replied. "I merely suggested the possibility of getting temporary assistance as the widow of an official who has died in the service. Also, your late father had been rather irregular in his job lately. Hence, the chances of financial assistance might be slim. Here, she is dreaming of a pension already. He-he-he!"

"She believes in everything from the goodness of her heart," Sonia replied. "You must excuse me now!"

"I haven't finished what I have to say," Luzhin stated. "Sit down. Seeing her helpless position with her unfortunate little ones, I wish to help her.

One can try to arrange a subscription or a lottery for her with the help of friends and outsiders desirous of helping such people in distress."

"God will repay you for it," Sonia replied.

"Maybe, but we shall finalise this. Come at seven o'çlock this evening. I hope Mr. Lebeziatnikov will help us. But I wish to warn you that it is unsafe to put the money in Katerina Ivanovna's hands. It is absurd that she has purchased Jamaica rum, Madeira and coffee for the dinner when she cannot make two ends meet."

"I don't know. It is only today...only once in her life...she was so eager to honour the memory," Sonia tried to explain, and then, burst into tears.

"I want you to accept a small sum of money from me with the condition that my name should not me mentioned," Luzhin declared, handing a ten-rouble note to Sonia. After Sonia left, Lebeziatnikov congratulated Luzhin for having done a noble and humane deed.

"A man like you who has suffered so much yesterday and still can sympathise with the

miseries of lesser mortals deserves to be congratulated. But tell me, what do you want with a legal marriage? Why is it so important in your plans?"

"That is because I do not wish to be made a fool of in your free marriage and raise another man's children. That is why legal marriage is my choice." Luzhin explained.

"Children?" Lebeziatnikov exclaimed. "I agree that children deserve first importance. But the matter of children has another solution. Why, some refuse to have children altogether! But the matter of honour is my weak point. It is nonsense to conclude that there will be deception in a free marriage. Why, a legal marriage has a higher probability of it. When the deception is open, as in a free marriage, chances of its existence are high. If I were to marry, legally or not, it would be just the same for me."

Luzhin sniggered, but Lebeziatnikov noticed that he was preoccupied in some other pressing thought.

Chapter Fifteen

A Mother's Death

Katerina Ivanovna was in a foul mood during the dinner. Most lodgers had chosen to stay away from the dinner just because Sonia would be present, as they did not wish to be seated with a woman of social disrepute. This promoted Katerina Ivanovna to be haughty and rude throughout the evening. She called the landlady, Amalia Ivanovna names like 'that owl' and snapped at the other guests. Amalia Ivanovna tried her best to ignore the insults. To make matters worse, someone passed Sonia a plate of two hearts pierced with an arrow, cut out of black bread. This agitated Katerina

Ivanovna, who called the sender, whoever he was, a 'drunken ass'.

The trouble between Amalia Ivanovna and Katerina Ivanovna finally erupted when the landlady got angry at the continuous insults and told her that it was long since she had paid money for her lodgings. Katerina Ivanovna asked Amalia Ivanovna how she could have demanded her lodgings yesterday when her husband had just died. The landlady retorted by saying that no wonder the ladies among the lodgers had refused to attend a party that was not hosted by a lady. The lodgers laughed loudly at this remark, goading Amalia and Katerina Ivanovna for a fight. The two women shouted at each other, and in the heat of the moment, Amalia Ivanovna shouted something about a 'yellow ticket'. Amidst the uproar, the children started crying as Sonia ran to restrain Katerina Ivanovna, who pushed her away to charge at the landlady. Just then, the door opened and in stepped Luzhin. Katerina Ivanovna rushed towards him. She urged him to protect her from this evil landlady.

"I do not wish to mediate with your everlasting quarrels with Amalia Ivanovna," Luzhin declared sharply. "I have come here to speak about my own affairs with your stepdaughter Sofya."

A stunned Katerina Ivanovna stood rooted to the spot as Luzhin walked to Sonia. The room had gone quiet. Raskolnikov, standing beside Sonia, made way for Luzhin, who barely noticed him. Lebeziatnikov did not enter the room, standing in the doorway and looking perplexed.

"Forgive me for the interruption," Luzhin stated to everyone. "Amalia Ivanovna, as mistress of the house pay careful attention to what I have to say. Sofya Ivanovna," he said, turning to Sonia, who was surprised and alarmed. "Immediately after you left my room, I found a hundred-rouble note missing from my table. If you know and tell us where it is now, I promise that the matter will end here. But if you do not, the consequences will be grave."

Sonia denied taking the money persistently, and Luzhin accused her of ingratitude for stealing hundred roubles even after he had given her a donation of ten roubles. Katerina Ivanovna took the ten roubles from Sonia and flung it at Luzhin's face.

"Here! Take your money," she shouted, as she turned Sonia's pockets out. "I shall search her myself. See, she has nothing."

Just then, a piece of folded paper fell out of Sonia's right pocket. Many cried out, as Luzhin picked up the paper, and unfolded it. He held it up for everyone to see. It was a hundred-rouble note.

"Thief! Out of my lodging! Call for the police!" Amalia Ivanovna screamed. "Send her to Siberia!"

Everyone exclaimed, except Raskolnikov, who stood watching Sonia silently, occasionally glancing at Luzhin. Sonia was transfixed, and

broke down suddenly, protesting that she knew nothing about the note.

"You are fools to think that she could have stolen that money," Katerina Ivanovna exclaimed. "She would sell her last rag to help you, and she has a yellow passport to stop my children from starving. She has a heart of gold and can never steal."

Everyone was moved to compassion at the state of this helpless woman, including Luzhin, who said he was willing to forget the matter now that he had his money back. Then, he glanced at Raskolnikov who stared back with fiery eyes. Katerina Ivanovna was hugging and kissing Sonia like a madwoman, and the children were sobbing as they embraced Sonia.

"How vile!" a voice sounded from the doorway. Luzhin turned around as Lebeziatnikov repeated his words.

"You are a mean slanderer," he said, striding towards Luzhin angrily.

"What do you mean?" Luzhin protested.

"I saw you putting that hundred-rouble note in her pocket as you escorted her out of the room," Lebeziatnikov stated. "I thought it was an act of kindness and did not mention it. Little did I know that you are so vile."

"It's a pack of nonsense," Luzhin protested, as everyone surrounded him.

"Call the police! I'll take my oath on it," Lebeziatnikov said. "I saw you pick up that hundred-rouble note from the table as you gave her the ten-rouble note. So, I was curious what you'd do with it."

"You have no evidence," Luzhin shouted.

"But I do," Raskolnikov stated quietly. In a firm and composed manner, he told the gathering how Luzhin had tried to defame Sonia in front of Raskolnikov's mother and sister and why Luzhin's marriage with Dounia had been cancelled.

Luzhin stole outside quietly and had left the house in half-an-hour. An upset Sonia left soon after. Amalia Ivanovna ordered

Katerina Ivanovna to vacate the lodgings immediately, and the latter ran away to seek justice. Raskolnikov followed Sonia home. He had to tell her who had killed Lizaveta and was in debate with himself about it.

"What would have become of me if not for you," Sonia said to him, as he arrived.

"You would have ended up in prison if Lebeziatnikov and I had not been present there," Raskolnikov said. "It is all because of the life you have chosen, which will result in the ruin of your family."

He suddenly felt a great hatred for Sonia just like he had felt for the old pawnbroker. His face must have reflected his feelings, as Sonia moved away fearfully from him. But his hatred disappeared like a ghost when he saw the love in her eyes.

"What's the matter?" she whispered.

"Nothing, it's all nonsense," he replied. "Don't be frightened, Sonia. Why do I torture you so?"

"Oh, how you are suffering!" she exclaimed.

"I've come to tell you who killed Lizaveta!"

"Have they found the killer?"

"No!"

"Then how do you know about it?"

"Guess!"

"Why do you scare me so?"

"I must be a good friend of the man who killed Lizaveta as I know," Raskolnikov continued. "He didn't mean to kill her. It was an accident. He wanted to kill the old woman, and when Lizaveta arrived there, he had to kill her too."

Sonia looked at him with great terror. "Have you guessed?" he asked.

"Good God!" she emitted a mournful wail and sank on her bed with her face in the pillows. After a while she got up and hugged him tightly. "What have you done to yourself?" she whispered. "There is no one in the world who is as unhappy as you."

"You won't leave me then, Sonia?"

"Never! I will follow you everywhere, even to Siberia!"

"Maybe I don't wish to go to Siberia yet."

"You rob and murder, and then give away your last farthing," she said wondrously. "That money you gave Katerina Ivanovna. Was it....?"

"No Sonia," he replied quickly. "That money was mine. I received it from my mother. I didn't touch the old woman's money. It's all buried in a yard."

"But why did you kill her then?"

"I killed her because I wanted to be a Napoleon," Raskolnikov declared. "It was like this: One day I asked myself- what if Napoleon was in my shoes and had to murder an old pawnbroker to further his military career? Would he have hesitated? Taking his example, I murdered her. You think that's funny?"

Sonia didn't think it was funny, and asked him to tell the story straight, without examples. "I killed the old woman for her money, so I could use it to further my education at the university without putting my mother and sister into further burden," he explained. "But

I admit that killing her was wrong. What am I to do, Sonia?"

"You must confess to your sin!"

"I am not going to Siberia, Sonia."

"But how will you live? What will you live for? What a burden to bear all your life!"

"I shall get used to it. But the police are on my tracks and will arrest me soon. Will you come and see me in prison, Sonia?"

"Oh, I will."

"I think it's better you do not come and see me in prison, Sonia."

Just then, someone knocked on the door. "May I come in, Sofya Semyonovna?" a familiar voice asked. Sonia rushed to the door fearfully to see Lebeziatnikov at the door. He informed them that Katerina Ivanovna had lost her mind and was beating up the children. Sonia rushed to see her immediately.

Raskolnikov returned home. *Maybe it will be better in Siberia!* he thought. His musings were interrupted by a visit from Dounia.

"I don't want to judge you for cutting yourself from us," she said. "But come and see mother sometimes. Whenever you need me, or anything from me, just call and I shall be there. Goodbye!"

"Razumihin is a very good man, Dounia. He is also capable of real love. Goodbye Dounia."

Later, Lebeziatnikov met Raskolnikov. "Katerina Ivanovna has taken the children," he exclaimed. "She has gone totally mad! She is rapping on a frying-pan and making the children dance on the streets. They are crying. She will be arrested by the police soon."

They rushed together to find Katerina Ivanovna shouting at the children, instructing them how to dance in front of the crowd. A helpless Sonia stood to the side. Katerina Ivanovna even beat the children, who were dressed up as street singers. Raskolnikov tried to persuade her to return home but failed. She was delighted when an old gentleman handed her three roubles out of genuine sympathy. A policeman arrived and asked her not to create a disturbance. He wanted to escort them home, but the scared children ran away at the sight of the policeman, adding to the ruckus. As Katerina Ivanovna ran after them, she fell to ground. "Oh, she's bleeding," Sonia exclaimed. "She's cut herself!" On careful examination, it was revealed that the blood was from her chest. It was clear that she was dying. She was rushed to Sonia's place. Her parched lips were covered with blood. "So, this is how you live, Sonia," she said, coughing and looking at the room. "We have been your ruin, Sonia. Now, take care of the children as I die in peace! The ball is over!"

These were Katerina Ivanovna's last words! The children screamed as their mother died. Raskolnikov was then joined by Svidrigailov. "I will make all the arrangements for the funeral," he stated. "I shall put the children into some good orphanage. Each will be paid fifteen hundred roubles when they come of age."
"The reason for such benevolence?" Raskolnikov enquired.

"Ah, you sceptic!" Svidrigailov laughed. "I told you I don't have any use for that money. This is an act of humanity. The dead woman was not a useless old pawnbroker, was she?" he said slyly. "She was a special woman. Now, we cannot let Polenka meet the same fate, can we?"

"How do you know?" Raskolnikov whispered. He was having trouble breathing. "I lodge here, just on the other side of the wall with Madame Resslich," Svidrigailov laughed. "I've heard everything! You have interested me greatly. I had told you we would become friends. You'll find that you will get along with me!"

Chapter Sixteen

Svidrigailov's Passion

Raskolnikov was in a crazy frame of mind now. He confused events that existed in his imagination with actual events. He fell prey to panic attacks, and constantly worried about Svidrigailov. The fact that Svidrigailov knew everything bore heavily on Raskolnikov's mind. They hadn't spoken about the matter after that, but Raskolnikov knew it was inevitable that they discussed what Svidrigailov wanted.

Porfiry Petrovitch paid Raskolnikov a visit and apologised for the hostility in the previous interview. "We must be more open with each other," he declared.

"The murderer has been found now," Raskolnikov stated.

"Yes, but Nikolay is not the murderer."

"Then who is?"

"Why, it was you" Petrovitch whispered. "You are the murderer!"

"I did not murder her," Raskolnikov said, like a child caught stealing.

"It was you, and no one else," Petrovitch said with conviction.

"If I'm guilty, why don't you arrest me?"

"I have no evidence against you yet, but I shall eventually put you in prison. I came to tell you that. I have a genuine liking for you. So, please don't look upon me as a monster. You should surrender and confess as your sentence will be lessened."

Raskolnikov refused, and Petrovitch gave him two days to think over the matter, after which he would be arrested.

Raskolnikov rushed to find Svidrigailov. Had Svidrigailov met Porfiry Petrovitch?

Svidrigailov was a man who repulsed him. He still had designs on Dounia and was befriending Katerina Ivanovna's children with some evil scheme in mind.

Then I shall kill him, Raskolnikov thought.

Raskolnikov finally spotted Svidrigailov in the window of a tavern. He rushed upstairs and warned Svidrigailov that if he had the same intentions for Dounia, he would be killed.

"I have the deepest respect for your sister," Svidrigailov stated. "My marriage with Marfa Petrovna was more of an arrangement. So, it was only natural that I should fall in love with such a wonderful personality like your sister. Avdotya Romanovna is such a delightful creature that it's impossible not to fall in love with her. I chose to look away initially, but would you believe that your sister took the first step of talking to me? No doubt, she had heard about the dark, mysterious rumours surrounding me. You've heard the same, I daresay?"

"Yes, I've heard you causing the death of a child and a footman from Luzhin. Is it true?"

"I beg of you to drop the subject," Svidrigailov requested as he continued, "When Marfa Petrovna spoke to Avdotya Romanovna about me, I think she was moved to pity. Now, pity in a woman is the most dangerous thing, as she will go to any lengths to revive the affected man from his vices. I was so much in love with her then, that I would have abandoned Marfa Petrovna, even killed her, if your sister had commanded me to. I would have married her."

"I believe that you still have designs on my sister."

"Nonsense," Svidrigailov said. "I can dismiss all your suspicions by giving you the news of my marriage. Madame Resslich arranged the match, obviously to make a profit herself. So what if I'm fifty and she's sixteen? She'll be the devoted wife I always wanted."

"I'm coming to your house to see Sofya Semyonovna," Raskolnikov insisted.

"She isn't there. She has gone with the children to an old lady of high rank, the patronage of an orphanage. Sofya is meeting the old lady at her hotel. But if I were you, I'd run off to America before they discover the murder of the old lady. I can help you with the fare!"

Raskolnikov refused, and they reached Svidrigailov's house to discover that Sonia was not there.

Svidrigailov parted from Raskolnikov and met Dounia after that. They arrived at Svidrigailov's lodgings together, where Dounia flung a letter on the table. "Your letter accuses my brother of a great crime. Explain yourself," she demanded. Svidrigailov told her how he had overheard Raskolnikov confess about his crime to Sonya from his lodgings. Dounia almost fainted in shock, and Svidrigailov comforted her. "We can still save him. I can send him abroad."

"I must go to him," Dounia flew to the door. "Why is the door locked?" she demanded.

"Sit down and let's discuss how to save him calmly."

"Can he be saved?" Dounia asked, sitting down.

"It all depends on you," he whispered with emotion, and Dounia drew back in alarm. "One word from you and I shall save him," a trembling Svidrigailov stated. "I have influential friends. I'll get him a passport. I'll arrange passports for you, your mother and myself. What do you want with Razumihin? I love you! I'll do anything for you!"

"Open the door!" Dounia ordered.

"I have lost the key," he said, with a mocking smile.

"This is an outrage," Dounia cried, running to one corner, and barricading herself with a small table.

"Outrage? I've taken measures so that no one is at home, including the landlady. Would you betray your brother? Besides, no one would believe you that you came to the lodgings of a single man unwillingly. How would you prove an assault?"

"Scoundrel!"

"Think about it. Your brother's fate hangs in your hands. I await your answer to be your slave."

Dounia pulled out a revolver.

"Why, it's my revolver, an old friend," he said, smiling maliciously. "Where did you get it? I see the shooting lessons I gave you in the country have not been in vain."

"It's not yours, it's Marfa Petrovna's revolver. You killed her! Now, if you move one step further, I'll kill you."

"What about your brother?"

"You can tell on him. You are a murderer yourself!"

Svidrigailov took a step forward and a shot rang out. The bullet grazed Svidrigailov's temple and hit the wall behind. He wiped the blood with his handkerchief.

"You missed! Fire again." He laughed and moved forward. She shot again but it missed fire.

"You didn't load it properly. You have another charge. Go on. I'll wait."

She threw away the revolver, and Svidrigailov held her by the waist.

"Let me go!" Dounia pleaded.

"You don't love me then?"

"No!"

"You never can?"

"Never!"

Svidrigailov gave her the key and asked her to leave quickly. Dounia escaped. Svidrigailov wetted a towel and washed his temple. He picked up the revolver and examined it. There were two charges and a capsule left, and it could be fired again. Putting the revolver in his pocket, he went out.

Chapter Seventeen

A Suicide

Svidrigailov visited Sonia at her home. "I might be going to America, Sofya Semyonova," he said. "This might be the last time we see each other. Your sisters and brother are well provided for, and the money assigned for them has been kept safely. Here, take the receipt for the bonds."

"We are all indebted to you," Sonia replied. "Please don't think me as ungrateful. But we don't need the money now as I can make my own living."

"The money is for you. Don't waste words over it. You will need it," Svidrigailov replied.

"As for Rodion Romanovitch, he has to choose between a bullet in the head and Siberia!"

Sonia started, and assuring her that he would keep the secret, Svidrigailov set off for another strange appointment. He visited his betrothed's house, told her parents that he had to leave Petersburg on urgent business. He gifted the girl fifteen thousand roubles as a pre-wedding present, kissed her, promised to return, and left.

Svidrigailov checked into a hotel around midnight. He felt feverish but could not get any sleep as image after image haunted him. Dounia's image appeared to be replaced by a dead girl lying in a coffin. She was only fourteen. She had drowned herself after her heart had been broken, her childish soul crushed by an insult from a man. After nightmares all night, Svidrigailov woke up in the morning, and went outside with the revolver in his pocket. He walked to reach a street with many houses. Svidrigailov stopped

before a big house with a tower. Behind the closed gates, stood a small man wearing a soldier's coat and a copper Achilles helmet on his head. Svidrigailov stared at him silently.

"What do you want here?" the soldier asked.

"Nothing, brother. Good morning."

"This isn't the place."

"I'm going to a foreign land, brother."

"To a foreign land?"

"America!"

"America?"

Svidrigailov withdrew the revolver and cocked it.

"This is not the place for such jokes!" Achilles exclaimed.

Svidrigailov put the revolver to his temple.

"You can't do that here," Achilles shouted. "This is not the place."

Svidrigailov pulled the trigger!

Chapter Eighteen

Crime and Punishment

That same evening, around seven, Raskolnikov visited his mother and sister. Dounia was not at home, but Pulcheria Raskolnikov was besides herself with joy as she welcomed her son. The good news was that Raskolnikov's article had been published in a magazine finally. "I can see that you shall be one of the leading men in Russian thought," she exclaimed. "Oh, to think that they thought that this genius was madness!"

The twenty-three-year-old Raskolnikov experienced that strange and bitter-sweet sensation every author has when he sees his work and name for the first time in print. Then, recalling all the inward conflict of the past few months, he flung the magazine away in disgust. "Promise me, mother!" he said. "Whatever you hear about me, you shall always love me in this same way!"

Poor Pulcheria's face reflected terror when Raskolnikov told her that he was going away. Reaching home, he saw Dounia waiting for him. He told her that instead of ending his life, he had decided to give himself up. "That's what Sonia and I were afraid of," Dounia replied. "Thank God you still have faith in life!"

They hugged each other in tears and said goodbye. It was hard for Dounia, as she loved him. *Oh, why do they all love me so!* Raskolnikov thought, as he left for Sonia's house. *If only I were alone and no one loved me! None of all this would have happened.*

Sonia had been waiting for him all day in terrible anxiety. Dounia had given her company, and the two girls became great friends. Then, an impatient Dounia had left for Raskolnikov's room. Sonia cried with joy on seeing him but turned pale again. She said a little prayer for him and gave him a wooden cross. "You have your wish," he said. "I'm going to prison. Why are you crying?" Suddenly, a thought struck him that Sonia wished to accompany him to prison. "Where are you going?" he exclaimed. "I'll go alone! Stay here. What's the sense of going in procession?"

When Raskolnikov reached the Hay Market, and bowed to the earth, he saw Sonia again. She was watching him, hidden behind a wooden shanty. It was then that Raskolnikov knew that it was destiny that Sonia would follow him to the very ends of the earth, wherever his fate might take him. Raskolnikov entered the police office to learn that Svidrigailov had committed suicide. Ilya Petrovitch also informed him that Zametov was no longer there. "I know nothing," he replied, when questioned about Svidrigailov. "I only came to see Zametov."

Raskolnikov exited the police station hurriedly to see Sonia staring at him, pale and horror-struck. He smiled an ugly smile, turned and went back inside. "Hullo! You are back again. What's the matter? Forgotten something?" Ilya Petrovitch asked. Raskolnikov tried to reply, but only incoherent sounds came out. "You look ill. Sit down!"

"It was I…" Raskolnikov began.

"Have some water!"

Raskolnikov refused the water, and said clearly, "It was I who killed the old pawnbroker woman and her sister Lizaveta with an axe, and then robbed them."

People ran up on all sides as Ilya Petrovitch had his mouth open. Raskolnikov repeated his statement.

Chapter Nineteen

EPILOGUE

Siberia

SIBERIA: A town on the banks of a broad solitary river, Siberia is one of the administrative centres of Russia. A fortress in this town has a prison where the second-class convict Rodion Raskolnikov has been confined for nine months. A year and a half has passed since his crime. The sentence had been softened because of his alleged mental derangement and his acts of kindness towards Marmeladov's family. Thus, penal servitude was imposed for only eight years.

Raskolnikov's mother fell ill at the beginning of the trial. It was a form of nervous breakdown. Razumihin and Dounia moved her to a small town near Petersburg, and they saw Raskolnikov in prison whenever possible, before the sentence was passed and they were separated. Sonia had made up her mind to follow the party of convicts in which Raskolnikov was despatched to Siberia, with the help of the money left to her by Svidrigailov. Raskolnikov could not argue, as both knew it was fate!

Dounia married Razumihin two months later. Razumihin pursued his university degree with zeal, after which he intended to settle in Siberia with Dounia to be close to Raskolnikov and Sonia. Pulcheria finally died of brain fever. Sonia continued to visit Raskolnikov in prison, making a living as a dressmaker in town. It perplexed Raskolnikov that all the convicts liked Sonia and were respectful towards her. Yet, most of them hated him and called him an infidel.

One day, Raskolnikov was at work in the river bank with two other men and a guard. The guard went with a convict to fetch some tools, and the second convict started putting the wood in the kiln. Attracted by the beautiful landscape, Raskolnikov inched closer to the river bank. Suddenly, he found Sonia next to him. He recalled how he had always treated her and felt ashamed. He did not know how it happened. He suddenly flung himself at his feet and hugged her knees, as if begging forgiveness for everything. Sonia knew now that he loved her more than everything in the world. Seven more years! They resolved to be patient.

The same evening, Raskolnikov tried an attempt at conversation with his fellow convicts, and they replied politely. Everything seemed to be changing now! Sonia was so happy that she was almost scared of this newfound happiness! Only seven more years! Both were ready to look at those seven years as seven days! Raskolnikov was unaware that this new life would cost him

great striving and suffering, and that he would have to pay dearly for it.

But that is the beginning of a new story-the story of a man's gradual renewal and regeneration, his passage from one world to another, and his initiation into a new unknown life. That might form a new story, but this one has ended.

About the Author

■ Fyodor Dostoyevsky (1821 - 1881)

The famous Russian novelist and author, Fyodor Dostoyevsky was born on 11 November 1821 in Moscow, Russia. He is best remembered for the classics Crime and Punishment and The Brothers Karamazov. The son of a doctor, he was educated at home until 1833. He pursued the career of a military engineer, but decided to become a writer after graduating as his love for literature was greater than anything else. His work explored the human condition and themes like psychology and existentialism. He belonged to a deeply religious family and was a religious man throughout his life. Crime and Punishment is one of his most popular novels. Fyodor Dostoyevsky died on 28 January 1881 in St. Petersburg, Russia, the setting of the novel, Crime and Punishment. He was at the zenith of his career at the time of his death, which was mourned by most Russians. The interest that his writings brought about in the rest of the world, has only increased in time.

■ List of Main Characters

Raskolnikov: He is the protagonist of the novel. Raskolnikov is in dire straits financially and is forced to give up his education. The novel focuses on his inner conflict and turmoil, over the murder of an old pawnbroker.

Sofya: Sofya or Sonia is Raskolnikov's love interest. She is forced to become a prostitute to support her family. Sonya is extremely religious and is instrumental in bringing about the transformation of Raskolnikov.

Dounia: She is Raskolnikov's sister. Dounia is beautiful, intelligent, proud, but also moral and kind. She is brave enough to break her engagement with Luzhin when he insults her family and fends off Svidrigailov's advances with a gun.

Svidrigailov: He is Dounia's former employer, who is still in love with her and believes that he can make her love him back. He is suspected of killing his wife and causing the death of others, the guilt of which prompts him to take his own life.

Razumihin: He is Raskolnikov's best friend. He battles his poverty by working harder and not by seeking other means. His name is derived from the Russian word 'razum', which means 'reason or 'intelligence'.

Luzhin: He is Dounia's fiancé, and is a narrow-minded, and self-absorbed man. He wants to marry a beautiful, intelligent, but poor girl like Dounia to control her.

Lebezyatnikov: Luzhin's roommate, Lebezyatnikov is a young clerk who propagates the "new philosophies" such as nihilism that are the rage of St. Petersburg. Despite being confused, immature and self-centred, he retains the basic human qualities that a man should possess.

■ Questions

Chapter 1

- 1. *Who was the young man? Why had he become a recluse? Whom was he avoiding and why?*
- 2. *Who was the old woman and why did the young man go to meet her? Explain in detail.*

Chapter 2

- 1. *Why did Sonia not live with her family?*
- 2. *Briefly describe what happened after Raskolnikov reached Marmeladov's house.*

Chapter 3

- 1. *Briefly describe what Raskolnikov's mother's letter stated.*
- 2. *Describe Raskolnikov's emotions after reading the letter? Why was he in such a state?*

Chapter 4

- 1. *Who did Raskolnikov have a confrontation with and why?*
- 2. *How did the policeman handle the situation? Explain in detail.*

Chapter 5

- 1. *Briefly describe Raskolnikov's dream.*
- 2. *What important message does the author try to give us through this dream with respect to animals? Explain in detail.*

Chapter 6

- 1. *Why do you think Raskolnikov wanted to kill the old pawnbroker? How did the idea first enter his mind?*
- 2. *Who was Lizaveta? Why did Raskolnikov kill her when he hadn't planned on doing so?*

Chapter 7

- 1. *Who was Luzhin? Why had he come to meet Raskolnikov?*
- 2. *Why did Luzhin leave Raskolnikov's house? Explain in detail.*

Chapter 8

- 1. *Why did Raskolnikov enter a restaurant? Whom did he meet there? Describe their conversation briefly.*
- 2. *Why do you think Raskolnikov went to the scene of the crime? Describe what happened there. Why was he thrown out?*

Chapter 9

- 1. *Who was Marmeladov? How did he die?*
- 2. *Why did Raskolnikov leave all his money for Raskolnikov's family when he needed money badly himself?*

Chapter 10

- 1. *What was the cause of discord between Raskolnikov and Dounia?*
- 2. *Why was Razumihin angry with Zossimov? Explain in detail.*

Chapter 11

- 1. *Why did Raskolnikov feel sorry for Sonia when she arrived at his house?*
- 2. *Who was Porfiry Petrovitch? Why did Raskolnikov come to meet him?*

Chapter 12

- 1. *What did Svidrigailov tell Raskolnikov regarding ghosts? What was the latter's reaction?*
- 2. *Why did Dounia break off her engagement with Luzhin? Why was Luzhin angry with Raskolnikov?*

Chapter 13

- 1. *Describe in brief the conversation between Raskolnikov and Sonia when he went to visit her.*
- 2. *What was the conversation between Porfiry Petrovitch and Raskolnikov? What was the strange incident that ended the conversation?*

Chapter 14

- 1. *Who was Lebeziatnikov? Why did Luzhin and he hate each other?*
- 2. *What were Lebeziatnikov's views on marriage? Are these views applicable in our society today?*

Chapter 15

- 1. *Why did Luzhin arrive at the funeral party even though he had not accepted the invitation?*
- 2. *Who exposed Luzhin's evil scheme and how? Describe in detail.*

Chapter 16

- 1. *What did Petrovitch advise Raskolnikov to do?*
- 2. *Why did Dounia come to Svidrigailov's house? What happened there?*

Chapter 17

- 1. *Whom did Svidrigailov visit after being rejected finally by Dounia? What did he say to them?*
- 2. *How did Svidrigailov kill himself? Why do you think he ended his life?*

Chapter 18

- 1. *Why do you think Raskolnikov decided to confess for his sin?*
- 2. *Describe the events that happened after Raskolnikov entered the police station till his confession.*

Chapter 19

- 1. *What was the term of Raskolnikov's sentence? Why was the term lessened if the offence was so serious?*
- 2. *What are your views on the title of the novel? Do 'Crime' and 'Punishment' go hand in hand? According to you, what is the main message that the author has tried to give us through this great novel?*